WOLFSHE

DYAN DUBOIS

Cover Design by Claire Flint Last
Author photo by Jentry Dryden

Luminare Press
442 Charnelton St.
Eugene, OR 97401
www.luminarepress.com

LCCN: 2020905191
ISBN: 978-1-64388-313-7

For Janam

CONTENTS

The Legend

As legend goes, the original healer girl had a miraculous birth, although no one witnessed it. Her story traveled through the forest, settled on drippy moss, and took flight over cold seawater that separated many islands…and yet it lived, intact, as if told for the first time by the original mouth.

Long ago, in ages past, the most respected elder of Far Up spoke of the Great Flood, how it came, and how the world clothed itself anew. Being a person of great importance, the elder received the story directly from Raven, who had heard it directly from the mouth of the Great Spirit Creator. Now hear Raven's account of the girl's destiny.

TREMENDOUS EARTH SHAKES MADE THE ISLAND WATER-ways churn. Beach sucked away to sea, and a great wave rushed toward inland mountains. The upturned sea spit out creatures that had never seen light nor land. A collective howl rose from mountaintops and shred pale wispy clouds into strips that fell and dissolved in the salty water.

The huge wave roared toward Spirit Mountain and pulled with it everything in its path: animals of the forest, tree hoppers, meadow grazers, birds of the air, and every human too slow to mount a canoe. Back into the watery depths they flowed. Quicker than lightning hurled across the sky, whole islands and peoples disappeared. Only a few survived.

The wave ushered a black-and-white whale, shimmering and beautiful, to the upland green forests.

Whale looked out at his home: the frothy, turbulent sea. He saw small fish, crabs, and many scared creatures flopping side to side, gasping, as Earth Mother tried to steady herself. Whale, hearing a high-pitched sound, looked up to the mountain peaks wondering, One of my kind? He spotted movement. Green sea snakes wiggled in seaweed-draped branches. Whale recognized the sound of fear. He tasted its bitterness in his mouth. He slithered and struggled, propelling his great bulk with his powerful tail fin through the tangled mud, moss, and broken cedar trees to reach the sound. He hoisted up and knocked the wiggling creature from its perch with one tail-fin swat.

Something fell onto his broad back. He felt a two-flipper creature run the length of him, falling…and falling again. The creature grabbed his fin, pinching with its grip. Whale looked at the dangling pest's black sea-kelp hair, flailing limbs—useless in water, he thought—and a body covered with dull brown scales, thinking, What is this? The creature's dark eyes gazed into his. Whale knew the look of fear. His heart sunk with sadness. The creature uttered familiar sounds, ones Whale had heard before when he had looked up at dark shadows gliding above and pointed spears had notched his flesh.

"Help me. I'm scared," the creature cried.

Whale studied the dangling mess and recognized a human girl. Her fear and sadness touched his heart like the moan of a mother whale for her missing calf.

     Dyan Dubois

Whale said to her, "I will care for you, but you must come and live with me in my world. Land is not my home. I will take you into peaceful depths."

The girl shook her head and said, "No. I breathe mountain air and light. I will die if I go with you. I am not your kind."

"And I am not your kind."

The great whale, seeing the girl shiver with cold and fear, thought for a moment. He remembered something his grandfather, the strongest and wisest whale of all, the conveyor of time, had once told him. His grandfather's voice rose on the water that frothed white in the distance.

You are of my lineage. We carry two natures. Our ancestors chose water…and land life. They gifted us a wolf heart and the power of the sea. In ages past, we changed at will from whale in the sea to wolf in the mountains, whenever we wanted. Now, if we change, we remain for a lifetime. We have the power although rarely used. Choose now; the sea rushes in again. The human girl will die. She has no water life. You have either land-wolf, or water-whale. Decide quickly! Once done, it's for your life.

Whale looked into the dark water of the girl's human eyes—full of fear—and caught a glimmer of light and hope. He felt his heart warm. He chose land. His great body flipped and thrashed in the upland moss and mud, tossing the human girl to the ground. A tremendous howl rose from his upturned head. He quaked. He contracted. The girl jumped out of his way and climbed a tree to avoid his massive fluked tail as it pounded the air and turned to fur. She heard water gush onto the green moss. She looked down. The wolf, shaking sunlit water droplets off his matted fur, gazed up at her. His gold eyes pierced hers. She trembled. She shut her eyes. When she opened them again, she saw kindness in his animal eyes.

Wolf yelled, "Look to the sea. Another wave charges. It will swallow us. Jump on my back. We will run to the mountaintop."

The girl saw the water, a frothing ridge on the move, coming straight at them. She shimmied down the trunk. The wolf crouched. She leaned in, grabbed handfuls of fur, and kicked her leg over the wolf's back. She steadied herself and bent low, burying her face in his neck mantle. The wolf bolted uphill, leaping over tangled logs, dodging shattered trees, soaring above bramble thickets. Up, up he raced to the very top of the mountain.

The great swell surged up the mountain, overwhelming everything in its path, crashing through ancient trees that for centuries had gripped the earth with deep roots. Their crowns, trembling, disappeared beneath the savage water. The wave climbed until it could climb no more. Dry rock and earth repelled the hungry water at the mountain top. It gurgled and sputtered and slid backward with a great sigh, dragging bushes like craggy fingers in its wake, rolling boulders like pebbles, sucking earth life down into the fathomless dark sea.

The girl slid off wolf's back to plant her feet on dry ground. She saw wolf's paw, ripped and gushing warm red blood. Searching trees for spiderwebs laced in their boughs, she grabbed handfuls of the sticky white strands, packed his wound with the fibers, and covered them with leaves. She pulled out strands of her long, dark hair to secure the leaves tightly around the wound.

"Rest now, wolf. You breathe with trouble. You must learn air. The sea has left you."

Wolf looked at her and nodded with understanding. When he caught his breath, he said, "I will be your spirit guide, your totem. You will be my healer. This I swear: in

     Dyan Dubois

every age of human life, a woman-child will be born with your healing knowledge, and in every age a wolf of my kind shall guard her. The ancestors promise that from Great Floods alliances will come."

⸻⸺◦⸺⸻

GREAT SPIRIT CHOSE RAVEN TO SPREAD THE WORD OF this agreement, his gift to human and animal. Raven carried the legend wherever he flew. He recounted the Great Flood promise from the watery edge of islands to far distant shores. Great Spirit entrusted Raven to speak the Truth and to prepare humans…for the cycle knows no end.

So, in every age Raven appears and presents a sprig of cedar to a newborn girl, signifying her special birth. Before the water rises.

CHAPTER ONE

Awakening

For two moons the air grew heavy with cloud feathers, soft but denser than usual. Blue sky gave way to silver rain that slapped the cedar boards of the longhouse roof. A lone wolf howled in the distance. The fire's warmth, the only comfort, provided a place of rest after a full day of medicine work. But this night felt different, not peaceful, to WolfShe. She watched as Ama stirred the broth and roasted lily bulbs. Even the quietness of the cabin and the pleasant aromas couldn't erase WolfShe's terror.

A loud howl ripped the bright morning sky. Wolves! Low, guttural rumbling filled the valley. Animal shrieks pierced the morning like arrows. A panicked cascade of whoops and screams rumbled up the mountain, bounced off crags, and echoed along the valley, spooking the elk and deer. Then life hushed. No gull flew, no dog barked, no human shouted, no elk bugled.

WolfShe felt the roar of death rake her chest. She tried to forget. She pushed away the memories, stuffing them into her moccasins, trying to lose them in the earth floor of the cabin, but they rose up and lodged in her forehead, burning with cold heat.

WolfShe relived the day her world fell dark. She could still hear her family's desperate screams gurgling in chaotic water when she closed her eyes. Did I scream, she wondered, when my hand slipped from mother's grip? She couldn't remember. She felt her mother's hand, cold and claw-like, disappear. She heard her father's deep voice leap through waves like a dolphin, yelling for her baby sister. WolfShe felt a sharp punch to her ribs. She choked. Her hair crawled down her throat; saltwater spewed from her nose and mouth. She opened her eyes to see her world upside down. Canoe shards impaled cedar trees. Cold mud squished up between her toes. She shimmied along moss-covered branches and fell onto ferns and sea kelp tubes. Struggling fish tried to swim in liquid brown earth.

WolfShe spotted a woman, her cedar skirt ripped to shreds, her face covered by mud-matted hair. The girl clawed her way through soggy forest debris to reach her.

"Maaha?" WolfShe screamed. She rubbed clumps of black hair away from the woman's face. Not my mother, she whimpered—not mine. But she recognized the woman, a shell trader from a nearby village. She watched the woman's spirit rise from the limp body like gray campfire smoke. *Poof.* She was gone. WolfShe watched hundreds of spirit bodies turn the blue sky gray, until she alone remained with the echo of their laments.

WolfShe shook her head to dispel the vision and tended the fire in Ama's cabin, shoving bits of charcoal with her stick, pushing the painful images away, turning the screams from her ears. She focused on the soft, orange firelight glowing on Ama's forehead, how it melted down the crevices of her cheeks. She took a deep breath.

"I know what you're thinking about, girl. I can tell from your eyes. That terrible day when Great Wave came ashore. Whales swimming in the stars. Whole tribes departing to the Land of Mists. Islands sinking. Saltwater shoving Salmon People into meadows, gasping for air. Seal People tangled in camas. I am sorry for you, girl, for your family, for your tribe, all lost." The old woman gently patted the girl's back. "Great Spirit spared you for a reason, WolfShe. Remember that."

"Ama, I don't want Great Spirit to keep me here. I want to be with my family. I have to find them. I remember so many spirit-body clouds rose to the sky. Some hovered for days looking down, searching with unfelt hands through the mud and branches, the dead fish and animals, for their loved ones. I covered my ears. Their shrieking—day and night—frightened me, kept me awake. They carried on and on until…one day their crying stopped. The silence was worse than shrieking. Like a huge cavern, it sucked me down to the world beneath the earth, where it's dark and cold. A black snake slithered toward me. I heard someone scream: *Rise!* I jumped up and swam to the water's surface. That snake still haunts me. He slithered and gulped down terrified spirits who had lost their way. I counted on my fingers: one, two, three sunrises. On the fourth, birdsong started at first light. I felt even more alone. Abandoned even by ghosts, I had no one to share the joy of birdsong."

"You saw spirits, girl? In your heart…or with your eyes?"

"Ama, as clear as I see you now, I saw them then. I heard their moans. I felt their pain."

"You have a gift, girl."

"For death?"

"No, for life."

      D Y A N D U B O I S

AMA STUDIED WOLFSHE'S WRINKLED FOREHEAD, HOW HER thick eyebrows touched at the center with worry, wondering what prompted her memory now after so many seasons?

WolfShe began. "Ama, I didn't have a way to tell you before. You grew words in my mouth. Like stinging ants, they ran over my tongue and around my teeth. I couldn't catch them. They didn't match what I saw and felt. Nothing did. But tonight…my heart breaks, and I can use your words. Memories flow like rushing water. I wish I had turned to spirit vapor and risen with my family, with my people. I wanted to. I begged to."

Ama sat back on her haunches and looked at the child she had raised, the child she loved, trembling and confused. She wanted to hug her, to sing to her, to rub soothing herbs into her brow, but she did nothing. Ama knew the flow must take its own course. Memories become enemies for life if they are rushed…or neglected.

"Child, Great Spirit wanted this. Why else would I have found you? These memories come now because your *woman time* approaches. Your breasts budded. Now your womb makes ready. This happens only once in a woman's life. With it, visions and remembrances come. Some are gifts. Some are challenges. All must surface. Do you dream?"

"Yes, Ama, as soon as I put my head down. My eyes shut to this world and open to another. Dreams appear like visions. They melt when I grab them. They're sticky like spiderwebs. But one dream doesn't melt in the dark of night, or the light of day."

Ama nodded in agreement and stirred the embers. "Soon your sacred place will bleed."

Ama knew her daughter would walk a new path now, the fierce path of knowledge, the way of the Seer. She would learn what Great Spirit requires of her and why she was spared. Ama had known for many moons that WolfShe would practice sacred medicine and continue her work. She did not know what perils that would bring, or if WolfShe had the strength. Several times she had looked through the mist to see WolfShe's future, but a curtain of gray forbade the vision. Why?

"We must prepare a circle-of-light blessing ceremony for you. You will fast and pray, purify your body and spirit."

"No, Ama. If sacred medicine brings dreams and visions, then I will not be a medicine woman. Terrible things live in darkness—like Black Snake."

Ama shouted, "There is no Black Snake! Those are your fears tricking you. I began your sacred medicine instruction four harvest seasons ago. I have watched you grow. You are gifted in treating illness, making cures, and understanding the power of medicine plants. But you understand nothing about yourself!"

Ama calmed when she saw WolfShe's temper flare like fanned embers. She knew she had touched a weak spot. And she knew that weak spot was WolfShe's early life, something Ama could do nothing about. Ama had wondered if Great Spirit had made the girl part animal. When she netted her that day, Ama felt she was not a natural Two-Legged. She ran like a wolf on all fours—bit like one, clawed like one— and had no words to fill her mouth, only grunts, hisses, and growls. Ama wanted to turn away from the berry patch, but the feral child lured her and scared her…if she were a human child. Ama couldn't leave the skinny thing in the wild. Great Spirit had made her, and she had found

　　　　DYAN DUBOIS

her…for a reason. She realized if she could make the child understand her sounds, then someday she could learn her words. Ama would discover her past and help her find her people, if they had survived.

Ama smiled, "You were a wild one. At times I wouldn't go near you. You clawed so much."

WolfShe looked down and whispered, "Ama, I don't know why you kept me."

"Because of your dark eyes, girl, they flickered with light. I thought if the flood hadn't washed the light out of you, and you had survived alone in the wild, then, I would see what you could become with my help."

"Girl, ever thought about the name I gave you?"

"No. I was wild like a wolf, so you named me WolfShe."

"True, but there's more. I figured you were saved by a she-wolf. I'd heard of that in a story from The Long Ago. I wondered why would a she-wolf suckle you when she could eat you? Wolf People don't raise Two-Leggeds. But maybe one had. So, I named you WolfShe, girl of the wolves."

"I like my name, Ama. Naming gave me who I am—not my totem, not my family—but who I am with you…because of you. Your wild daughter."

Ama slowly lowered herself by the fire next to WolfShe. She sat in silence. Her breathing slowed. Ama's head slid down to her chest, her hair a silver curtain over her shoulders. She sighed like a dark night with no stars or moon. WolfShe giggled. She touched Ama's shoulder and ran her small hand down Ama's back. Warmth like a sunny beach day traveled from WolfShe's hand down Ama's hunched backbone. Ama looked up, wiping water from her eyes, to see WolfShe swaying with her eyes closed. She seemed far away on a spirit journey, but her hand remained fused to

Ama's back. The old woman smiled. WolfShe jerked away and collapsed on the dirt floor, her knees sticking up from her tunic like knobby sticks. She grabbed them close to her chest and rocked back and forth, whimpering like a pup.

"Ama, you pushed me down."

"No, WolfShe, I didn't. What you felt came from you, not from me. When you couldn't take the heat, you pushed away. It's a sign. Fire is the purifier. Great Spirit calls you… healer."

WolfShe panted like someone who had run up a mountain. She rolled to her side, clasping her hands to her chest. Ama placed a blanket on her and patted her back. "Rest now, girl. Stay warm by the fire."

⟨ơ/ơ/ơ⟩

WHEN WOLFSHE WOKE, SHE SAW AMA ASLEEP ON HER mat on the opposite side of the firepit. Dull orange flickers from the dwindling embers played on the cedar boards of the cabin. A basket of soup, still warm, rested on the rocks. WolfShe helped herself to the mushroom and fern-tendril broth. When she quietly stepped outside to relieve herself, she saw a stark, black-and-white world chiseled by the glow of the full moon. Illuminated white branches wrestled with low-lying black shadows that crawled along the ground. WolfShe stood in the calm, cool air. She inhaled the rich smell of damp earth and cedar.

A shadow moved. WolfShe held her breath to listen. The dark form froze. "Who moves in the night?" she whispered. "Raccoon friend?" WolfShe knew the smell of broth lures night visitors, but this felt different. Another movement. She surveyed the cedar boughs hanging low to touch the ground. She leapt into the cabin, pulled the cedar-slat barrier across the entrance, and secured the antler-bone hook. She stoked the fire. Gold sparks rose to the opening in the plank ceiling. For some reason, this night visitor seemed different. WolfShe didn't know why. She pulled her blanket around her shoulders and sat up for the remainder of the night, positioned between Ama and the door, listening with her flint-blade knife gripped tightly in her hand. Something lurks outside, she was sure. But what?

Dawn light crept around the cabin door and woke Ama. WolfShe heard the old woman's knees crack when she stood. Ama jerked when she saw WolfShe sitting upright, knife in hand.

"What's wrong?"

"I couldn't sleep. I thought I saw something last night."

"What?"

"Something black moving in the tree shadows. I don't know. Something that didn't run from me."

"Did the black thing smell?"

"No."

"Good. Evil always smells foul. Easy to recognize, like rotting fish. Your woman change brings power, wakes you, scares you, teaches you. You learn true from false. That's why we have a ceremony, so your spirit awakens to the power of the Creator and chases evil away. You saw a night traveler, probably a raccoon. They love mushroom broth. No evil can come to our cabin. Blessings live deep in this cedar. I see to that. New morning sun calls. Fetch our baskets. Today we cut camas, collect herbs."

⊰※⊱

WolfShe looked across the field at Ama—bent, old, ropey like cedar roots—her arms moving back and forth, cutting camas faster than WolfShe could. Ama: the only person she thought of as family, the only person she loved, the only person who loved her…on earth.

But WolfShe's mother, father, and sister in the Land of Mists pulled her with unseen hands. For her, they remained out of reach. She could touch, hear, and communicate with Ama. Aware that memories of her family weakened like a lake reflection in evening light, WolfShe feared they would disappear altogether and abandon her.

WolfShe struggled to preserve the few memories she recalled, but that final memory rushed in and separated them when the cliff of water roared onshore. Earth slipped under sea. Cries punctured the air, yet no gull squawked, no dog barked. The chief bellowed: *Now!* Braves aimed their canoes toward the mountain, looking behind as the wave blotted out the sun. Families crouched on floorboards. WolfShe dug her nails into the wood. She smelled fear. Boats shattered on impact, sounding like thunder. Red-brown cedar shards speared the gray water. People somersaulted in the turbulence, screaming and gasping for air. WolfShe's world fell dark.

WolfShe wiped her eyes. She saw Ama's silver-thread hair sparkling in the sun as she methodically cut, bunched, and moved to the next clump of camas. WolfShe had never thought of Ama as old, but now, when she looked at Ama, she felt like she'd fallen into an icy stream. She couldn't imagine not grabbing her hand, talking to her, listening to her stories. WolfShe stopped cutting to stare. Is Ama shorter, or am I taller? She moves like a heavy basket rides her back. She watched Ama pause, grimace, and wrench her back upright, shake her hands in the air, open and close her knotted fingers—the same deft fingers that wove baskets

          Dyan Dubois

tight enough to hold water, strong enough to carry heavy loads, wise enough to make medicines.

WolfShe ran to her. "Ama, let me finish. You worked hard yesterday preparing cedar bark; your hands must be tired. Besides, we have enough camas. I'll cut the bear grass. You rest. Let me do the knife work."

Ama lowered herself to the ground, landing with *uuh*. "I'll sit a little, watch you work," she said to WolfShe. WolfShe grabbed bear grass with her left hand, sliced with her right. Ama chuckled. "Looks simple when you do it, girl. How are our winter stores? Signs for a cold, damp winter are here. I checked the elderberry patch, not ripe. We'll make extra honey-elderberry syrup. Bearberry too. In the upper meadow, we'll collect wild ginger and mint under the trees for stomach decoctions. Still need to scrape scrub pines to start the resin running and get spruce pitch. So much to do."

"Don't worry, Ama. I can handle the chores. You enjoy your weaving."

"We're low on wormwood leaves too."

"I've already picked them. They're in the drying shed."

"So much wound dressing last spring, we almost ran out of supplies."

"Yes, Ama, when those two whaling canoes crashed on the rocks, twelve men needed splints and poultices." WolfShe worked as they talked, blade in hand, sweat shining on her brow, feet firmly planted in the warm earth. She looked at Ama and swallowed hard. "Are you feeling well?"

"Mid-sun's very hot today," Ama said, wiping her face. "I'll return to the cabin for a rest and bring smoked salmon back for you when it's cooler."

"Ama, I'm not hungry. I'll return at sunset. You go now."

WolfShe watched Ama make her way over uneven ground using her knotted, yellow-wood stick, the one the tribe had gifted her at the harvest potlatch, until her small frame disappeared into the trees across the meadow. Returning to work, grabbing and cutting, stacking and packing, WolfShe settled into a rhythm, hardly stopping to stretch.

A noise caught WolfShe's attention. She paused. Ravens? Ama's totem sounded upset. Shading her eyes, WolfShe watched seven ravens carve large circles in the sky over her head, their late afternoon shadows running along the ground like phantoms. Ravens talked—not to her—only to Ama. But she hoped one day to speak with Raven People. Ama told her ravens choose when and to whom they speak. WolfShe decided they didn't speak to her because they weren't her totem, even if Ama wanted them to be.

WolfShe heard branches snap at the forest edge. She paused. The ravens overhead squawked like women clucking their tongues in displeasure. WolfShe studied the forest shadows. The ravens screeched a long, high-pitched *aihhhh* and scattered. Thundering hooves erupted from the trees. A huge bull elk charged WolfShe, his herd close behind. WolfShe grabbed her empty basket and waved it overhead. She jumped, whooped, and yelled. The buck and his herd careened to the right and disappeared down meadow.

WolfShe's weight shifted; she rocked side to side. She saw meadow grass wave without wind. A rapid jerk knocked her flat on her stomach. She tossed onto her side, then flipped to her stomach again, clawing the trembling ground. She heard the earth roar. Another quick, hard jab threw her into the air. She crashed to the ground, the wind knocked out of her. She prayed to Earth Mother. The ground trembled like a scared child. WolfShe got up on wobbly legs. She saw ravens flying sideways in the sky. In the distance, she heard the bull elk scream a blood-stopping bugle that made her skin crawl like stinging fire ants. Trees groaned and crashed. Branches snapped. The earth ran sideways, pulling her with it. She tumbled and saw with cinched eyes; she heard; she remembered.

⸺◦◦◦⸺

My parents crashed against the cedar boards of our longhouse. Father grabbed my newborn sister's cradle. Mother crawled to me. She crouched over me, wrapped me in her damp, cool arms. Drops of blood from the gash on her head dripped onto my forehead. I felt her beautiful blood, how it joined us. I knew then we would never be separated. Not Ever. We rolled sideways, Maaha and me. Her heartbeat slapped my face.

Screams of women, children, elders, and animals filled the gray, sticky air. I tasted fear, bitter as wormwood. We stumbled outside; Mother dragged me by the hand. Father threw baby sister, strapped in her cradle, on his back. From Sister's brown eyes pools of water fell. They slid down Father's back, silently. I knew those tears robbed Father's courage; they cut through him like a knife. His skin turned ghost-white like ice. I remember the sound Maaha made, like an animal giving birth and dying at the same time, like an elk I'd seen. The calf lived. The mother didn't. That sound, raw as unripe berries, seared my throat.

⸺◦◦◦⸺

WolfShe watched smoke spiral up the fire hole of the cabin. She heard the hearth fire crackle and spit. The aroma

WolfShe   17

of stewing fish and seaweed made her mouth water. She swallowed hard and noticed the last rays of sun drop below the cabin entrance. The dull orange pricked her eyes like pine needles. Ama's lush, green meadow faded gray. WolfShe looked up at Ama waving a cedar bough over her, chanting.

"Ama, what happened?"

"You're bruised, girl. You did well. Our longhouse held, rocked, didn't split. But our medicine hut needs repair, roof fell in. How you made it here so fast, I don't know. Earth Mother spoke, not a whisper, a shout. I started to you as fast as I could. When you reached me, you asked if I was hurt. Then you fainted. Great Spirit protected us, Daughter. I fear others have wounds. Drink this soup. I must carry medicine baskets to the village. Can you go?"

"Yes, Ama. Let me sit a little."

"You ran like the wind. Your feet didn't touch the ground."

"Did the sea come in?"

"No, child. Earth Mother stretched and settled. No wave."

"Did you hear Raven People?"

"Yes. Elk People ran so close to our cabin they kicked mud onto our boards."

"They ran at me making horrible shrieks. The hair on my neck stood up. Bull elk led his family away from the forest. I heard trees cracking."

"Drink this, girl. I've gathered poultice salves, cedar bandages, and needles. Be strong. You look like a witch chased you. No color to your face. No warmth to your touch. Scared to death. You should rest. I will go alone."

"I saw a memory from when I was little. There was a hard shake. Maaha, Father, and my newborn sister..." WolfShe looked at the clearing in front of the cabin. She

 DYAN DUBOIS

thought she saw something dart between the trees. "No, I'm coming with you, Ama. Something's out there."

The old woman stood at the cabin door, scanning the landscape. "Only a raven shadow tangled in branches."

CHAPTER TWO

Coming of Age

WolfShe prepared for her coming-of-age ceremony, fasting, joining the women's sweat lodge, and attending prayer circles. She had never spent much time with others. She knew since childhood they had whispered about her. Many commented on the scratches on Ama's hands and arms from taming her, and how the feral girl could make animals obey her, even the wildest. She scared them. They kept their distance. She kept hers…until now.

WolfShe enjoyed hearing the women talk about their men. A new world opened to her. She had sisters…and they had stories. Not only stories, but valuable information, deep ways of understanding the female body, its gifts and spirit. She had thought only her Ama wise, but now she realized every woman carried wisdom, some great, some small, as a birthright. Without women, men would be lost, the circle of women told her. That reassured her. WolfShe assumed that her mother must have guided her father and baby sister to the Land of Mists, unless Black Snake had gulped down their spirits before they reached the gate, a thought she couldn't face.

At a sweat lodge meeting, a woman told a story about Great Spirit asking what Raven thought of male Two-

Legged creation. Raven cocked his head to the side, tapped his beak on a clamshell, and replied: *All they do is fight.* So that's why Great Spirit created female Two-Leggeds, to teach males how to work together. When WolfShe walked home from the lodge that night, she wondered if she would ever have a male companion. She shrugged. Would I want to?

The sweat lodges introduced WolfShe to new ideas and knowledge, but they opened a door inside that she did not want opened. WolfShe couldn't shake the feeling that scared her, the same one that surfaced when the meadow cracked. Starting as a circle of darkness, it uncoiled and spread through her like black sap, blanketing pleasant thoughts, sweeping her veins with coldness and loss. Then black ooze would shrink and coil into a circle of darkness again…and leave her alone. Earlier, she had named the ooze Black Snake as a way to control it. To name is to control, she believed. After all, having learned Ama's words had given her a productive life based on naming, yet she had no more control now than before when it came to this enemy.

⸺⟨ა/ა/ა⟩⸺

WINTER BROUGHT SNOW TO THE SANDY SHORE. JAGGED Peak Mountain shimmered like a mysterious spirit, shrouded by clouds. Fierce, cold winds blew across the meadow, snapped huge limbs of ancient cedar trees, and muffled desperate howls. WolfShe wondered, What makes Wolf People uneasy? Why do Raven People fly far? Do they sense Earth Mother's unrest, how she turns and twists to find comfort? WolfShe felt the tremors when others did not.

When she walked in short-light days, WolfShe heard a low, constant hum like a beehive in summer, but no bees traveled in winter cold. One day, the increasing sound made her misstep. Her foot slid out from under her on the icy path. Her head smacked frozen ground. The chapped, dry skin of her lip split wide. Everything sparkled like stars in the night sky, lost their light, and disappeared. In the darkness, WolfShe saw Black Snake. His large, scaled body curled around the obsidian pond that glowed with a silver crescent moon held by the black water. His tail flicked back and forth, a gray halo distinguishing his curve.

Black Snake hissed: "Look upon my darkness; enjoy my power. When all else falls away, you only exist here… with me."

WolfShe heard a woman scream. A wolf howled. She struggled to stand.

⌘

"Child, hold still," Ama shouted. "One last stitch. There, done." She slathered spruce gum over the stitches and pressed cedar-cloth on the wound to stanch the bleeding. "Hold this ice on the bandage until the pain numbs." Ama stepped out to toss the basket of bloody water onto the frozen ground. She returned to see WolfShe gagging. She grabbed WolfShe's left hand and pinched the webbing between her thumb and first finger. WolfShe slumped back against the wall, snatching gulps of air, until her breathing regulated. "Girl, the wound is shallow, only three stitches. No cause for all this."

"The hissing, the howling in my ears. The black…"

"Howling? Those wolves are far from here. I hardly hear them. Suck on these leaves. They'll make you sleepy."

"No, Ama. I don't want to sleep. The snake will get me."

Ama looked at the girl's wild eyes. "What snake? Spit out that leaf. It's too strong for you. Take a sip of this willow bark tea." WolfShe shied from Ama's hand. She spat words that clumped together, skipped spaces, and made no sense. Ama wiped the tangled hair away from WolfShe's forehead, propped her up on her sleeping mat, and covered her with two dog-hair blankets, wedged along her sides for support. "There is no snake, WolfShe. You hit your head. Glad I was getting more wood. You could have frozen out there."

"Stay with me, Ama. Sit here beside me."

"Rest. I'm here. Tip your head back a little to rest on the wall. The lip won't swell as much. When you wake, the pain will be gone." Ama smiled at WolfShe. "You're safe, girl. Sleep and heal. Sip this again. I won't leave you."

WolfShe closed her eyes and stared into darkness. She felt something cool and slimy like kelp rub her leg. She couldn't move away. She heard a wolf wail. The howling drew closer. She felt warm breath on her face. WolfShe's running heart slowed; her erratic breathing calmed. She smelled sweet ferns and moss-covered logs on damp animal fur. She slept.

When she woke, it felt as if from a tiring day of field work. She heard Ama humming outside—her weaving prayers. Making baskets in the morning chill, not good for Ama's hands, WolfShe thought. She pulled herself upright and folded the blankets to the side. She stood, wobbled, found her balance, and walked toward the entrance.

Ama turned to see her braced in the cabin door opening. "Up so early? Any pain?"

"No, Ama, no pain."

"Come. Let me see your lip. Tight seam, little swelling. Good. You took a hard fall. Wrap up, get your broth, and sit in the morning sun while I prepare Sitka sedge for my new basket."

"Aren't your hands cold, Ama?"

"Not yet. I enjoy morning sun…even in chill air. Winter fades. Soon willows will bud and swell. We'll celebrate you at Swelling-Bud Round Moon.

"Ama, what if I'm not ready, not prepared, not cleansed?"

"WolfShe, you are ready. You have doubts?"

"Yes. Something evil lurks in me."

"Evil?" Ama leaned over and inhaled a long breath of WolfShe's scent. "You're as sweet as spring meadow flowers. Don't worry. Woman change has spooked you. You don't know what to expect. You have fears. Changing from girl to woman brings doubts. They fade. Visions come. You will learn your life's duty."

"I thought you already *knew* my life duty, Ama. You said I would be a healer, a medicine woman, like you."

"Yes. I see that and more. You determine what more. I teach only what I know. The healing way is not the end. It is the beginning. You will find out."

"What? My totem?"

"If we knew your ancestors, we would know your clan's totem. Mine—Raven—I've seen speak to you, but you don't respond. A totem calls to you, guides, instructs, and protects. A totem links you to your ancestors, now and in the spirit world. I haven't seen that you listen…yet."

"Does anyone have Black Snake Totem?"

Ama gasped and laughed so hard she dropped her basket. "No! Black Snake doesn't live. I heard of him, the trickster, from an old tale when I was a child. He lived below the ground, in darkness, luring innocent children to join him. Do not speak of Black Snake. WolfShe, what you hold in your thoughts and heart rush to your mouth. Once spoken, words are as strong and binding as bark on trees. Do not allow a black snake to speak to you."

"Yes, Ama," WolfShe said, wanting to cry out, *But I've seen Black Snake and heard his words. He scares me.*

BEFORE HER COMING-OF-AGE CEREMONY, WOLFSHE'S FAT lip healed. A fine line curved the thickness of her bottom lip, making a shallow indentation where the lip had split. She knew the location without looking. Each time she licked her lips, she felt a tiny ridge tingle. She studied the lip in a water reflection. She decided she liked it. She noticed her face had changed. Soft baby cheeks had become prominent cheekbones with gentle hollows below. Her straight hair now had gentle waves. WolfShe liked what she saw. She stirred the still water into ripples, so her thoughts would fade with her face. She knew no good comes of staring at one's reflection. Because…sometimes you see beyond.

WolfShe felt her ceremony would reveal a secret, one she needed to honor. She had heard the song of bumblebees in winter. Surely a sign. Next would arrive the important message. Her coming-of-age ceremony would bring it, she was sure. She hoped a whisper from the Land of Mists would tell her where to meet her family…and when. She longed to see her mother, father, and sister. She wanted to find her own people and become Medicine Woman of her clan totem to honor them and to receive their blessings and their promise to meet her in the Land of Mists when her time came.

HER WOMANHOOD CEREMONY CAME AND WENT. STILL no message. WolfShe felt no older, no wiser. She'd been blessed with prayers and healing incantations and had received gift baskets, a cedar box inlaid with iridescent abalone shells; a rain hat waterproofed with elk oil; a sacred eagle feather; an elk-bladder water carrier, but her most treasured gift came from Ama—an etched sea-otter tooth. Ama had worn it around her neck for as long as WolfShe could remember. The incised black lines had lost some of their inking, but the design, a prayer, remained. Ama's teacher had given her the amulet for strength and protection. Now she passed it on to WolfShe.

Soon after the ceremony, Ama warned WolfShe: "Do not attempt to contact your mother in the land beyond. The amulet you wear is powerful. You might interfere with your mother's spirit. Just outside the Land of Mists, lost souls cling to the gate and try to snag the living by making ropes of well-wishes. They tie up the wisher and climb down to earth to attach to a living body." Ama repeated in a loud voice, "WolfShe, do not ask Great Spirit for impossible blessings. Do not call your mother's spirit out."

WolfShe listened, but she felt she knew better. Communicating with her mother was possible and necessary. She needed to make sure her family had passed over together. She needed to learn her family totem. She feared Black Snake might trick her if she couldn't declare her totem. She needed her ancestors' protection. The time to contact them must be auspicious. She felt now, with so many blessings upon her, would be the time. She respected Ama. She realized the power of her words, but Ama had no idea how the evil Black Snake haunted her. Without her own totem's knowledge, WolfShe feared Black Snake could defeat her. His ooze could cloud her mind, render her weak, and drag her into his dark underworld forever.

     DYAN DUBOIS

WolfShe intended to hold a private ceremony to transport her into the Land of Mists to search for her family. She kept her plan a secret…for Ama's protection.

⸺◈⸻

MANY LONG-DAY SUNSETS DROWNED IN THE SEA WHILE WolfShe worked, making potions and poultices, gathering and sorting plants, and plotting. She realized she must first rid herself of Black Snake before attempting to reach her family. Otherwise, Black Snake could snare them at the gate.

"WolfShe, you've been quiet since your ceremony. Don't lament childhood's passing. New things await you. Every stage of life has beauty…even old age."

WolfShe wanted to distance herself from Ama to guard Ama from Black Snake's probing. She grimaced. "Old age, beautiful? I hear your swollen joints pop when you bend. You limp on rocky trails, even with a walking stick. You forget stories you've told me, so you tell them over and over. Your chest gurgles, even in dry weather. What's beautiful about old age, Ama?" As soon as she'd spoken, WolfShe's heart sank. She knew the power of words, effective as blades, but more damaging. WolfShe wanted to protect Ama and make her withdraw for her own safety. "Ama," she said placing a firm hand on Ama's bony shoulder. "I spoke with fire, but you leave me no other way. I am my own person now. I have come of age. I listen to me now."

Ama looked up at WolfShe but said nothing. WolfShe sat down beside her, picked up cedar strands strewn around Ama's feet, and began weaving.

"You've learned many things, girl. Your talent for herbs, everyone remarks on. Your neat hand stitching, no one can beat. Your strength of body…But I worry about your strength of spirit. I feel something pulls you down."

"Only you, Ama. You don't let me grow up. You taught me your skills. I am strong…in all ways. You must trust that."

"But your heart…frost clings to the edges and creates a fern pattern that pushes people away. Only you can heal your heart."

"I know. Ama, I will rid myself of that."

"Use your healing gifts for others…and for yourself. Don't seek revenge. I've seen this fire in you since I took you in. Your anger flares like deer grease on flames. What was done, was done. You can't hold a log in the river's flow. You will drown. You lost everything you loved, yet Great Spirit kept you here. Heal yourself, so you can heal others. Entire tribes sunk into the sea. It wasn't the first time. It won't be the last. We work according to Great Spirit's plan. When you question old age, WolfShe, you question Great Spirit's plan. Yes, old age brings stiffness and pain, but it brings something you cannot have in youth."

"What Ama?"

"The ability to see backward…to understand. You are busy making memories. I am busy understanding them." WolfShe fumbled with cedar strands, twirling them around her finger in tight curls. Ama stood; her knees and hips popped as she straightened. "Well, girl, you can't say I'm silent in mind, or body."

WolfShe grinned. "No, Ama. I always know where you are."

Ama smiled. "Today I will walk to the riverbank to sit with the women who repair salmon nets. What do you do?"

"Go to the forest. I need moss bandages. Plus, I hope to find honeycomb. Will you return by night, Ama, or do you stay over with your family?"

"Too much for one day. I will stay in the village. Will you join me?"

"Ama, I'm a grown woman now. I need to finish my medicine herb collection. I will stay alone here. You stay at your sister's."

"Will you be afraid? You haven't stayed alone at night."

"Hoot owls don't scare me. Besides Bear People will follow you, waiting for salmon."

Ama smiled. "Close those entrance boards before dark. Keep a good fire. I will return before sunset tomorrow."

WolfShe watched Ama amble down the path with her sleeping mat tied to her basket, her shawl wrapped tightly around her shoulders. She stood and rested her hand on the antler rack she'd made last shedding season for Ama, so she could dry her clothes near the fire, and rubbed her finger along the bumpy antler spikes, pledging to Great Spirit: *I will give Ama something far better than this rack. I will destroy Black Snake's evil.*

WolfShe felt a chill run down her arms; hairs stood up in tiny bumps on her arms. She looked around the cabin. In the far corner she saw a slight wave, possibly a crack in the wood that caught a fire glimmer, she thought. She turned to go. A tail eased out of the shadow, slithering side to side. WolfShe grabbed the antler rack from the wall. She stepped closer. The movement receded, becoming motionless in the shadow. Black Snake. But how? Nothing evil could enter Ama's cabin. Ama had told her so. WolfShe sniffed the air, but only woodsmoke with the remnants of broth lingered, nothing foul. She wondered, could Ama be mistaken? Could a medicine woman make a mistake, misjudge evil for good, or good for evil? She began to shake. If Ama could, then anyone could—especially her. She lunged forward and slammed the antler points into the corner. Her hands shook from the impact. Nothing stirred. Nothing was there to stir. WolfShe inspected the corner and felt sick. Black Snake was capable of traveling beyond the obsidian pond like a shadow. He might appear anywhere, anytime, even here, a sacred place. WolfShe ran to the drying hut and pulled down sacred herbs to cast a barrier blessing. She put the herbs in each corner of the cabin and across the entrance. Since he hadn't spoken to her, or taken full form before he disappeared, WolfShe knew Ama's protections had weakened Black Snake but not prevented his shadow access. She sang protection incantations and vowed to destroy him.

⁓∿∿⁓

WolfShe prepared for work, feeling confident her incantations held. Walking the path to the woods, her thoughts drifted back to the first time she had tasted honey. She found a chunk, clotted with decayed bark strands, on the forest floor. When she reached down, the waxy clump stuck to her fingers. She sniffed. A sweet aroma like dried meadow grass and flowers made her mouth water. An amber ooze ran down her fingers. Her tongue rolled over the sweetness, separating it from embedded sprigs of moss and decayed cedar. Sunlight and flowers exploded in her mouth. She squatted on her haunches, plunged her tongue into the clump, and devoured the chunk of honeycomb, spitting out white clumps that balled between her teeth. She hummed, licking the gooey ball from her fingers. She had never tasted anything like it. WolfShe wanted more. She looked up at the gray, noisy haze that circled the branch high above where sticky sweetness lived. She tried to climb the trunk but couldn't reach the first branch. Her fingers clawed pieces of bark. She lost her grip and slid down, hitting the ground. She knew from that day that those fliers around the branch had something special, something she wanted very much, and she intended to get more.

Ama had taken WolfShe back to the hive days later. She tried to teach her the words for Bee People and their sweet ooze. WolfShe understood the taste but not Ama's words. Ama made a buzzing sound, pushing air through her puckered lips, moving her head in circles. For many summers, WolfShe made the buzzing sound, tilted her head, and pointed to the forest when she wanted Ama to take her for honey. WolfShe named the sweetness *uzz-uzz*, a sound that sharpened to a whistle at the end. She still heard her word for honey, *uzz-uzz*, when she thought of honey.

WolfShe realized as she approached the trees, hoping to gather honeycomb for Ama, that she could hear the bee sound whenever she wanted by remaining quiet, even with no hive near. She thought this must be a coming-of-age gift from Great Spirit, and soon she'd hear every creature's sound woven together: Raven People, Wolf People, Salmon People, Bee People, Elk People, Whale People, every Two-Legged and Four-Legged. And their song will taste sweeter than honey. She licked her lips in anticipation.

Walking the damp forest footpath, turning over rotten logs to find mushrooms, searching for succulent fern roots to roast, gathering moss for wound dressing and bedding, she didn't notice the daylight fading. Shafts of light in the tangled leaves weakened. She looked up. Above the ancient cedar, she spotted the first dim star. She knew Ama would not like her being out so late, alone. WolfShe lifted her basket, cinched its strap across her forehead, and drew her knife from its sheath. She didn't feel afraid, but Ama had trained her to carry her knife in-hand in low light and to study signs along the way.

Cool air settled on the forest litter. WolfShe wrapped her shawl around her and picked up her pace, a running walk, not wanting to upset her full basket. She realized she had walked deep into the forest, but she should have cleared the edge by now, or at least be able to see it. She couldn't. She thought to Ama: Ama, I stayed too long. Can you see me? Where do the trees end? Can you hear me?

She heard only her dog-pant breath. She hoped to hear Ama say, Child, walk this way, turn here, walk straight—but she didn't. She promised Ama she'd never say a mean thing again and would always listen, if she would guide her now, speak to her now. No reply. A drizzle began. Cold droplets slid down her face. WolfShe shivered. The forest hushed and grew darker.

WolfShe crouched near a downed, hollowed-out tree trunk. She threw pebbles in. She jabbed inside with sticks. Nothing growled, nothing hissed. Rain started in earnest. Ground mist swirled among black, lacy ferns. She backed into the log on her stomach, leaving her basket outside at the entrance to block animals seeking shelter. The dank smell of rotting wood made her nose tingle. She shivered and attempted to wrap her shawl around her shoulders in the cramped space.

WolfShe felt relieved, knowing Ama would be away from home tonight. Ama wouldn't worry about her. She would assume WolfShe was warm and safe in their cabin, on her mat next to the fire, warming soup on the hot rocks… as promised. WolfShe could reach home by early dawn and make a fire. The embers would still be warm when Ama walked in. Everything would appear normal. But WolfShe felt disappointed in herself. Ama had taught her: Girl, be aware of your surroundings; read the signs. WolfShe hadn't. She had gotten absorbed in memories and forgot to watch her way, and the light.

Rain pelted down, the first hard rain since spring. The drops sounded like fat squirrels jumping on the rotten log. She dosed. Later, when night sounds woke her, forgetting where she was, she tried to get up. Her head slammed into soggy wood. She stayed awake a long time, listening, but finally fell asleep and dozed lightly.

A shriek cut the night air. WolfShe jerked awake. She held her breath and tilted her head to listen. The cry came again, a wail of shock and pain that rumbled through the forest, rousing birds and animals. Wolf? she thought. Her body shook. The animal's fear wrenched her heart. Something's killing that wolf. But wolves have no enemies in these woods.

The yelping, crying, howling, snarling grew increasingly frantic. Wolves far up-mountain echoed a faint howl. He's dying, WolfShe knew. She wiggled out of the log on her belly and stood upright in the rain. She could outrun a dying animal, she figured. But what then? She couldn't listen to the animal suffer without trying to help. She reached for her knife and medicine basket. She crept through the trees, moving toward the sound, walking hands-in-front to protect her face from unseen branches. Stiff bracken crunched underfoot. She held the knife blade between her teeth, ready. Clouds separated above the tree canopy, allowing insipid moonlight to seep through and drip down the branches. She saw a dark, writhing body in the distance. She lowered her medicine basket and traced a large arc around the dying animal. The wolf attempted to stand. He snarled but collapsed with a shriek, spasmed, and fell motionless.

WolfShe saw something by his foreleg glowing dimly in the broken moonlight. She remembered Ama had spoken of a trap, unlike anything her people had seen, with strong teeth a knife could not cut. She recalled an elder had shown her a hard, sharp-toothed trap that glowed orange in fire but did not burn. He had found it in the woods. Wolf's leg must be caught in such a trap, she thought. His spirit will soon rise and turn to vapor if he doesn't get help.

She grabbed supplies from her medicine basket and edged closer to the wounded animal but stayed out of reach. She slathered a leaf with devil's claw salve coated with honey, rolled it into a ball, and tossed it near the wolf's mouth. He didn't move. She drew closer. A wild animal in pain was dangerous and unpredictable—she knew—especially a dying one. A wolf's instinct to survive is powerful. Using a stick, she eased another wad under the wolf's snout. He clamped down on it. WolfShe jumped back. He tore the ball open and gummed the goo dripping down his lip. She squatted and watched. He finished one ball of salve. She made another, adding more devil's claw for pain. She tossed it near his mouth. He swallowed the clump whole. She tossed a third. He caught the wad in the air and gulped. Good, now you'll sleep, she whispered.

She waited. The wolf's body fell slack. Crouched out of range, she prodded him with her stick. He didn't react. She poked him hard in the ribs. No response. Holding very still, she listened to his breaths, uneven and weak. She removed her store of dry cedar shavings and her flint to make a fire. When the flames rose, she passed her knife blade through them several times. The wolf remained motionless.

WolfShe knew she must work fast. She moved closer to study the wound. The hard teeth had bitten through the paw, leaving a bridge of crushed bone and flesh caught in the trap. She threw her shawl over the animal's head. If he woke, he'd be confused—she hoped—long enough for her to jump out of the way. She prodded again. He didn't react. She laid out strips of cedar bindings, slathered the first two with wound salve, and crouched over the animal. With a quick movement, she sliced the shattered bone and flesh from the trap. Blood flowed. The wolf trembled but did not wake. She tied a strip tightly around his leg to stanch the bleeding, repeating until the binding held the leg securely. She packed moss on the nub to cushion the wound, then added layers of cedar dressing until his entire leg, nub to shoulder, was protected. The wolf stirred. Lying on his side, he clawed the earth with his hind legs as if running. She pushed the last wad of pain medicine under the flap of his gums and jumped away. He attempted to move but fell slack again. She sat at a distance, listening. His breath slowed to shallow inhalations like a child's dreamy sigh. She had done all she could. WolfShe returned to the hollow log for her gathering basket and climbed a nearby tree to wait… and watch. The wolf remained quiet. She slumped in the crook of a large branch, leaned her head back on the hairy trunk, and dozed.

WolfShe woke with a jerk when her foot slipped. She caught her balance. Silver-gray dawn light crept among the tree branches. She stretched and looked down at the wolf. She blinked. She hugged the trunk and stood. She saw nothing. The wolf had lived through the cutting. But she feared he had slinked away to die, hidden, as wounded animals do. She knew he couldn't run. He could barely walk. She shimmied down the tree to inspect where he had lain. Using a stick, she pushed the trap up against a tree, paw flesh still dangling. Death jaws, she groaned. She buried the trap and dragged a log to cover it.

WolfShe spotted three paw indentations in the undergrowth. WolfShe's eyes watered. She whimpered, with relief and fear, he lives…for now. In the growing light, she recalled Ama's words: *If you fear you are lost, pause, think. The path is often near. Study your surroundings. Panic makes you turn in circles. Look for the straight path.*

Tears rolled down her cheeks. She wouldn't want Ama to see her like this: lost and afraid. She climbed the tree again. From her perch, she studied the ferns, downed logs covered with moss, towering trees touched by dawn light, and thought back to where her feet had touched ground. She realized she had turned away from the path where the immense two-trunk cedar she called the Twin Braves met the ferns. Looking for a hive deep in the forest, she had not studied the ground and lost her way. She backtracked. She saw a glint of pale pink light on water. She walked toward the stream, followed its course downhill, and reached the ancient two-trunk cedar. There she saw her own prints and followed them.

WolfShe burst into the chilly cabin, relieved to find it empty, grabbed sticks, and made a fire. After washing her hands at the spring, she returned, wrapped the duck-feather and dog-hair blanket around her and stretched out on her mat. The fire blazed bright, and the sun shone through the cabin door while she slept.

"ARE YOU SICK, GIRL? SLEEPING IN DAYLIGHT?" AMA SAID, shaking WolfShe by the shoulders.

"What? Oh, Ama, you're home." WolfShe glanced out

the cabin entrance at late afternoon light glowing gold on the meadow grass.

"Girl, the sun touches the sea. Are you ill?"

"No, Ama. Tired."

"Where's your wound?"

"What wound, Ama?"

"Blood on the door."

WolfShe jumped up, lost her balance, teetered, and righted herself against the cedar wall. She grabbed the door frame, leaned out, and looked at the dark stains. "Something terrible happened, Ama. A wolf was injured, bitten by hard teeth. He didn't hurt me. I tried to help him. That must be his blood."

"Here, at our door, a wolf?"

"I found him in the woods. Hard teeth bit his front paw, wouldn't let go. The bone was crushed. I gave him medicine for pain and sleep. I couldn't save the paw. I cut it from the trap and bandaged his leg. I climbed a tree to watch him. But when I woke, the wolf was gone. He suffered, Ama. I was his only chance."

"You stayed alone, at night, in the forest? You took a big risk, girl. He could have killed you. Animals in pain are vicious. In return for your help, what would the wolf do? He'd come here and eat you!"

"I gave him enough medicine to make him sleep for two nights, I thought."

"Where were the teeth that bit him?"

"Near a tree, in the woods, under moss." WolfShe looked at Ama's grimaced lips pulled tight over her teeth. She thought, Ama don't slap me. "I disobeyed you. I'm sorry." When Ama moved closer, WolfShe braced for the blow.

Ama stared at her. WolfShe saw a look she couldn't decipher. She knew she had disappointed Ama, but Ama kneeled in front of her and clasped WolfShe's hands in hers. She touched them to her forehead.

"Great Spirit spared you, girl. You could have stepped into that trap, and no one would have found you in time. I don't know what this means for the wolf, but I do know what this says for you. Twice saved. Another sign. The wolf came to our cabin to show he survived; you saved him. I will host a potlatch to announce Great Spirit decided your totem: Wolf."

"How do you know, Ama?"

"You lived. The wolf lived."

"We don't know if the wolf lived, Ama. He may have tracked me here and bled to death doing it."

Ama brushed WolfShe's matted hair back from her face. "He will return to…"

"What?"

"Wolves never forget, not a kindness, not a cruelty. You saved his life. He knows this. But do not go out alone, WolfShe, and never after dark. There are more dangers out there than wolves. As medicine woman, you will learn the truth of my words…and obey."

"Yes, Ama."

"Comb your tangled fishnet hair. I will make food. We eat dried salmon tonight to give you strength, roasted bulbs for healing, and your favorite—*salal* cake."

"Thank you, Ama, but why celebrate when I used so many of your cedar bandages?" WolfShe expected a stern reply, knowing how much work went into beating cedar bark to make pliable bandages.

"Well, girl, we celebrate you, but you do have work in the morning. You beat more bark. I'll make salve. We'll see who is faster."

CHAPTER THREE

Medicine Woman

Cold days came early and ruined the final harvest. Wind howled. Freezing rain flooded down the longhouse roof into the drainage ditch. But Ama, with joy, greeted three tribes who had come to celebrate WolfShe's medicine woman naming potlatch.

WolfShe, feeling shy and awkward, sat quietly and accepted their gifts of food, shells, feathers, cedar clothing, herbs, ointments, and talismans. With her head dropped low and her hands clasped tight, she listened to Ama recount the story of finding her adopted daughter, once a starving little girl without words—now a medicine woman—eating berries in the last hot days of summer, alone, with hair matted like rope, twisted around twigs, and clotted with mud, her scent wild as a fawn's, and her naked body scorched dark by summer sun. WolfShe sunk into her tunic and couldn't look up. She wished Ama would stop.

Ama recounted how she had watched the child, without her knowing, for two days before she decided she had no mother. She prepared to catch the feral child by braiding together fishing nets, and on the third, she waited for the child to come eat berries. Ama approached from downwind, without a sound, and threw the heavy net over the child who clawed, kicked, and bit, making sounds like a wounded animal. She had red welts, thorn scratches, and oozing blisters all over. Ama wondered if she'd been stung by yellow jackets or rolled in nettles. Ama knew the girl could die if the sores became infected. She needed medicine. She needed food and shelter. But it wasn't easy to drag her home.

Ama tossed a lily bulb coated with sleeping powder into the net and watched the girl sniff and gobble it. Ama pulled the growling, netted girl home, keeping her distance from the child's small teeth and long claw-like nails. She tied the net to a tree by her cabin and washed the girl with baskets of warmed water, continuing to offer her roasted lily bulbs through the mesh.

Ama fed her until the girl's small tummy swelled and her eyes shut. When she slumped over on her side and breathed slow, even breaths, Ama untied the net. The girl didn't stir. Ama cleaned the blisters and applied poultices and carried the girl to a mat where she wrapped her tightly in a blanket for the night, tying one foot to a post.

Ama figured she'd lost only two milk teeth, but said with a grin, "I learned that day which pain is worse. Thorn or milk teeth. It's not thorn." At the laughter, WolfShe dropped her head even lower on her chest until Ama motioned her to sit up straight. "But here she is tonight at her naming ceremony as your new Medicine Woman of Wolf Totem."

An elder from Jagged Peak Mountain clan chanted the blessing. He whisked cedar smoke around WolfShe and pronounced in a loud voice: "Great Spirit bless our Medicine Woman of Wolf Totem." Ama tipped her head to alert WolfShe to stand and face the people. The audience erupted in whoops. He continued, "I saw three-paws wolf on the path." The elder looked directly at WolfShe and said, "You cut the front right paw off that injured wolf to save it?"

"Yes, Honorable One."

"He moves fast. A beautiful animal, dark like charcoal, gold eyes that watch everything, know everything. He carries power on three legs. His spirit is strong."

WolfShe stood quietly. She assumed the elder saw the wolf she had helped, but she wasn't sure. She couldn't imagine the animal could run. She nodded and said, "He is strong then."

"Like the wind, he is there and not there. Does he call your spirit, Medicine Woman? Do you wander to meet him?"

"Honorable One, I haven't seen him since he was caught in that trap."

"He hasn't called to you? Wolves are powerful beings, favorites of Great Spirit. Be aware. Their power can make you forget. They are spell weavers. Not all spells are good. But you, as medicine woman, would know that. We can only assume Wolf is your totem since your people are lost to us. But that three-legged wolf stands and runs, proof in my opinion, his spirit claimed you. Be wise in dealing with him."

The old man ambled away to greet family members. WolfShe sat down and stared at her lap to avoid eyes on her. She wished Ama would come to her. But Ama talked to her sister. A brave approached and stood in front of WolfShe, waiting for her to look up; she did not. He reached for her hand, turned her palm up, and dropped a beaded necklace into it and walked away. WolfShe remained still, feeling the warmth that radiated from the beads, like spring sun after a harsh winter, she thought.

Strong north winds blew. Lashing rain pounded the earth. Muddy rivulets ran in longhouse ditches. The season of coming together in feasts to chat, weave, tell stories, exchange gifts, and rest made the long, cold nights enjoyable. WolfShe's summer of preparing medicines, gathering and drying food, storing firewood, and collecting cedar, sedges, animal hair, and feathers for winter weaving faded in the warm glow of communal fires. She could sit, listen, and enjoy, although she knew the cold wet winds would soon bring illness.

She reviewed her checklist of preparations and cures: cedar bandages, plenty. Camas, harvested. Death lily, dried and marked. Chewing gum, softened and wrapped in clumps. Cough-plant leaves, dried and layered. Cascara and mint stomach tonics, powdered. Hog-fennel smelling salts—she smiled—enough powdered to wake up a sleeping village. Chokecherry, enough for fifteen spring births. Willow bark for pain, dried and powdered. Deer and elk grease ointments, two baskets full. Spruce-gum wound dressing and wood splints, plenty. WolfShe could relax now, she hoped.

After the council declared Wolf as her totem at the first potlatch of short-light season, her credibility increased. Her new title Medicine Woman of Wolf Totem made her feel good, but WolfShe knew many whispered, *witch*, and the three-legged wolf was proof. No real wolf could survive death-teeth to run fast on three legs. Only a spirit wolf could, a *demon* spirit wolf, a wolf from the land of darkness, they whispered.

WolfShe knew she couldn't depend on respect from the tribes in the same way they respected Ama. They will give

       Dyan Dubois

me credit for my healing skills, that's all. I am not one of them. An approaching brave interrupted her thoughts. She kept her head down and nibbled at the last bite of salal cake on her wooden plate. Another payment for my services, she assumed. At her feet lay balsam root, sarsaparilla, woodpecker feathers, and shells. She didn't look up. Receiving gifts made her uncomfortable.

The brave cleared his throat to get her attention. "Medicine Woman of Wolf Totem, a traveler has come. He joins our potlatch. He has an important message for you. I will walk you to him."

"I can see him alone," she said glaring at the brave towering over her. Had she seen him before at her potlatch? Did he drop a necklace into her hand, a gift for the new medicine woman? She wasn't sure, but his stare made her skin turn bumpy like a toad's. She felt her body chill. She stood. "Keep two paces behind me."

When she approached, the messenger said, "I travel from Green Valley Village to honor you and ask that you and Raven Totem Medicine Woman come help us. An elder is sick. He suffers illness of wind. Breath won't visit his chest. Tomorrow, his grandson arrives to guide you."

"Yes, we will go to him. Enjoy our feast tonight. Show him where to sleep," she ordered the brave and disappeared before he could follow her.

In the purple morning, WolfShe heard someone at their cabin door. She looked out, nodded, and left him waiting in the cold, while she walked to Ama's corner and pulled her curtain back. Ama opened her eyes.

"The brave waits outside."

"Ask him in, girl. Stoke the fire. Offer food. That's no way to greet a guest."

WolfShe walked back to the door, opened it, and pointed to the fire. "Come…sit." She studied the dirt floor, how snow fell from the fur of his elk boots. She heard his leathers sigh when he crouched to warm his hands by the fire.

"I will walk you," he said with a voice like dark earth warmed by the sun.

Ama, lacing her boots, peeked out, and motioned her over. She whispered, "Girl, give him warm broth. You look like a scared rabbit. I know his mother, father, and grandfather well. He is no stranger. He's Running Bear."

"Cold. North wind snow coming," he said when WolfShe handed him broth.

WolfShe knew it was cold; she felt the snow coming; north wind brings snow. He tells me what I know, she thought. He thinks I'm stupid. He's the stupid one.

Ama walked in and broke the uncomfortable silence. "Running Bear, welcome. My daughter, WolfShe, doesn't remember you. You played as children." She shot a sharp look at WolfShe that made her straighten her back. "How long has your grandfather been ill?"

"Five sunrises. He's getting worse, gulping for air like a fish on sand."

She turned to WolfShe, perched in the far corner, picking through leather packets of herbs. "Bring aged honey, cough-plant, and our winter medicine baskets. We must reach Green Valley before this storm."

"Yes, Ama."

"And cut two cedar boughs for ceremony."

"Yes, Ama," WolfShe said and grabbed her knife.

"I can," Running Bear said. "It's cold. I'll cut the boughs.

  D Y A N D U B O I S

You stay warm."

"No! It's our sacred tree, not yours." WolfShe glared at Running Bear. He looked down, a sinew in his jaw twitching like a bowstring.

"Thank you, Running Bear, but WolfShe says a blessing prayer before cutting, our sacred chant. You stay by the fire. She will return soon."

WolfShe yanked on her boots and shawl and bolted out the door, glad to be away from the brave. She trotted across the crunchy ground to the stand of cedar trees, wondering, What was he thinking? Besides, he smells. I've never smelled anyone so strong. He's like smoked salmon, cedar logs, and summer sun on blackberries. No one should smell like that. Ugh.

WolfShe whispered prayers to Great Spirit and stepped into the cedar circle. She looked up at the huge trees, their crowns eaten by the heavy sky. A chill breeze made their limbs sway. She closed her eyes. She felt the trees welcome her.

WolfShe said her healing prayer: *May the elder walk in health. Great Spirit and Ancestors guide our hands. Protect us on this journey. Keep us in your blessings.* For an instance, when she opened her eyes, WolfShe saw a glow, a soft pearly light like the sheen of a shell. She sliced off three small boughs and walked toward the cabin, cradling the cedar. Even in crisp air, the scent of cedar filled the night.

Her breathing slowed; her feet grew heavy. She stopped, rooted like a tree, yet her body swayed like a bough teased by gentle wind. Tangled branches made sounds like women chanting. Twigs snapped. WolfShe jerked and stood erect, knife-in-hand, to study a glow that formed a large wolf. Her breath caught in her throat and hardened like a winter lake. She couldn't utter a sound. Unflinching gold eyes watched her. She looked from the wolf's head to his short foreleg. "Three paws," she gasped. "Healed, not killed, Wolf Brother? Great Spirit blessed you."

The wolf stood perfectly balanced on three legs, watching. He touched his nose to the ground, sniffed, and moved closer. She smelled damp fur laced with fire smoke. His black neck mantle made him look much larger than she had remembered. But he had been lying flat, she reminded herself, and a season has passed. He wears winter fur.

His front right leg extended down, as straight as the others, but ended abruptly in a knot. He cocked his ears forward, listening. WolfShe felt no fear. She stepped closer. He remained in place. He didn't flinch. She took another step. He hop-stepped toward her. WolfShe stopped. She studied a remnant of cedar binding tied to his leg. Above, the flesh sagged like a bag of water. The bandage had to come off, but she would have to stoop close to his mouth level. She knew he could snap her neck in one bite.

She cleared her throat. "Wolf Brother, your wound healed, but your leg swelled. I must cut the bandage away. I saved you once. Let me help you again."

She didn't know what to expect. The wolf remained motionless, staring. WolfShe moved close enough to feel the animal's warm breath on her outstretched hand. The wolf didn't flinch. She kneeled beside him. Slowly she lifted her knife, edged the blade under the wrapping, and sliced. Wolf quivered but stood in place. The dirty bandage fell to the ground.

WolfShe stepped away from the wolf, sat back on her haunches, and studied his eyes. He tilted his head, sniffed, and turned, trotting into the forest where he melded with tree shadows. WolfShe felt elated and very cold—like ice, not blood, filled her veins. She stuffed the piece of blood-stained bandage into her tunic and ran.

"Girl, I just asked Running Bear to go out and look for you. What happened?"

"Look, Ama. I have boughs, good ones, hard-to-reach ones. Powerful. Blessed." She almost looked at Running Bear but didn't. "No need to send him."

"Let's go. The storm will worsen. But we have the best guide. Running Bear is known for his tracking skills. He is our strongest brave."

WolfShe made no comment, thinking, *not better than me*. She hoisted her baskets up, secured them at her forehead, wrapped her shawl around her, and stomped out the door. When Ama demanded she hand over one basket for Running Bear to carry, WolfShe acquiesced, biting her lip.

Running Bear walked in front in silence, carrying the cedar boughs and one medicine basket. Ama glanced at WolfShe, saying nothing, but she felt Ama's censure. She wanted to explain, but not with *him* around: The brave smells. I've never smelled a scent like his. Maybe he will hurt us? That's why I'm not friendly…to protect you, Ama. WolfShe cast her gaze to the uneven ground and marched beside Ama, ready to steady her if she misstepped, ready to stab him if he did.

When something moved to her right, weaving through tree shadows, she watched the halting, moving, appearing, disappearing. WolfShe blinked. Snowflakes melted in her eyes, warping her vision. She wiped them away, half expecting to see the wolf. She didn't. She walked on, head lowered, hair falling onto her face like a warm blanket, hiding her disappointment. Why did Running Bear have to come? Wolf won't show himself because of the stinking brave.

When they arrived at Running Bear's village, they followed the glow of longhouse cookfires to the last one. Running Bear trotted ahead, shouting. His mother stepped out to greet them as Ama and WolfShe approached. She hugged Ama and led her inside by the hand. She nodded and patted WolfShe and directed them to mats by the fire, ordering family members to stand up and vacate their places.

"Long time since the last visit," Ama said, "potlatch two harvests ago. How is your father?"

"Wet, choking cough. Weak."

"Take us to him."

"Both?"

"Yes. WolfShe, my daughter, is Medicine Woman of Wolf Totem. She makes powerful healing with hands and herbs."

Running Bear's mother bowed slightly in WolfShe's direction. She walked a few steps to pull aside an animal hide curtain and led them to the corner where the old man lay, his head propped up on a blanket, his body weighed down by three. Warming rocks surrounded his feet.

Ama greeted him. He slowly opened milky eyes but said nothing. She chanted a healing prayer, leaning down to his chest. "The sea moves in his chest. He's drowning. WolfShe, prepare breaking waves decoction," she said. WolfShe withdrew a handful of leaves from her medicine basket.

"Let me do that for you," Running Bear's mother said. "You stay with father."

Ama said, "WolfShe, tell her how to prepare," and resumed chanting.

WolfShe felt uncomfortable ordering an elder but instructed her: "Boil water, add leaves. Let sit, count two hundred deer, strain leaves, bring medicine to Ama."

Running Bear's mother left to prepare the drink. Ama looked at WolfShe. WolfShe knew what that meant. She removed the salve from her bag, put a clump in her palm, and rubbed her hands vigorously to warm it. The cold elk fat softened.

"You listen from his back, girl."

WolfShe pulled the loose drape aside and pressed her ear to the old man's upper back. She nodded at Ama and whispered, "Cold waves, crashing water." Ama motioned her to come in front and listen to his chest. "Squeaks like a mouse. Heartbeats like pebbles hitting soft ground."

"What would you do, WolfShe?"

WolfShe realized Ama asked her…not a question but a plea. She hardly knew how to reply. She sat quietly on her haunches and asked Great Spirit. She opened her eyes. "Break wave by force. Wind will enter."

Ama nodded in agreement. Ama positioned herself in front of the elder, bracing his thin shoulders. WolfShe took his back. She rubbed heating salve up and down with broad, deep strokes. The old man groaned. She whispered to him. She slapped hard between his shoulder blades with the side of her hand. Her small hands moved up and down his back, beating his flesh like a stretched animal skin. She stopped and rubbed salve along his neck and down his shoulders. She braced his weight against her, reached in front, followed the lines of his level shoulder bones, and dug her fingers in between the shoulder and the outside tip of the bone. She pushed and released. She repeated the pattern several times, making the old man whimper like a whelping dog. The water in his lungs sloshed. With eyes closed, he screamed: "Wolf! Wolf! Run!"

Ama stared at WolfShe. WolfShe kept working, sweat

trickling down her wide eyebrows. She grabbed his shoulders, pulled them back, and pushed them forward until like fish gills they fluttered. She stopped and motioned for medicine tea. Running Bear rushed in with the warm, smoky drink. WolfShe held the tea to the old man's mouth and made him drink the bitter brew. He grimaced with every sip but obeyed. She began again, pushing, shoving, rubbing salve, listening to his chest, administering medicine tea.

Finally, WolfShe lowered the man onto his mat and covered him with blankets. She ordered Running Bear to bring hot rocks and position them at his grandfather's feet and near his chest. WolfShe collapsed against the wall boards, dripping with sweat. No one spoke. Ama softly chanted and swished an eagle feather over the elder. He rallied, yipped, and cried out "Wolf, wolf, wolf" and fell asleep.

Running Bear's mother ran in, crying. Ama looked at her. "Your father has not departed to the Land of Mists. WolfShe gave him breath. Her totem chased demons away. He rests now. He no longer swallows cold sea. Keep him warm with hot rocks, day and night." Ama handed a cedar bag of wormwood to his daughter. "Make him drink all day, hot tea. When he improves, give cough-plant to chew. WolfShe, speak," Ama said looking at her daughter with respect.

WolfShe did as she commanded. "He must breathe scrub-pine sap. Warm and rub sap on cedar cloth; place under his nose. Keep it by fire rock, so you all breathe scrub pine. After two sunrises, he will strengthen. Feed only broths, then smoked salmon and roots."

His daughter looked at the medicine women. Tears filled her eyes. She put her hand on WolfShe's arm. "Father cried out *wolf, wolf, wolf.* Why?"

Ama answered. "Great Spirit sent a wolf-spirit vision to make grandfather run, so his chest would fill with air and scare the demons away. He won't remember his cries… or his vision." Ama continued, "My daughter, Medicine Woman of Wolf Totem, healed him." She whispered something to WolfShe before speaking again. "My daughter will sleep by him tonight. Make her mat. He will spit out the sea because of her treatments. I am old and tired. I will sleep by the fire. Running Bear assist my daughter."

Hearing that, WolfShe grimaced at Ama. How could she? Ama knows I don't like being left with others. I have no need of Running Bear.

"Running Bear will do as WolfShe orders," his mother said. "We will place a feather mat for you by the fire. You honor us with your presence. Come, eat with me while my son prepares the bedding. We can visit."

Ama and Running Bear's mother talked softly, alone in a corner of the longhouse. Ama told her she feared WolfShe would never gain respect because of her early years, living as a feral child in the wild. She knew many suspected the child had been born to a mother who couldn't, or wouldn't, care for her, a mother who had traveled far from her home to abandon the baby in a remote place where she would perish without shaming her mother. A child no one wanted must be a cursed child, people whispered, but Ama said she believed the girl had survived the Great Flood. Only Running Bear's mother had supported Ama in those early years. She had been her close friend since. When she heard gossip about WolfShe, she stopped it, so Ama wouldn't hear. People whispered how could the girl have landed in our woods from the Great Flood? That wasn't possible. Running Bear's mother would reply: Do you doubt our wise medicine woman? Has she not saved you from illness? Ama believes in the child. I believe in Ama. Watch your tongues. Serpents strike their owners.

Ama confided in her friend that when she first found WolfShe, the child acted like a wolf cub, scratching, snarling, biting. Ama wondered if she were human or a demon in disguise, so she put salt on her tongue to test her. Demons hate salt. She rubbed salt all over the struggling child. The girl growled and licked her skin. That convinced Ama she was no demon, only an orphaned child.

After eating, the house grew quiet. Ama said good-night to her friend and stretched out on the sleeping mat by the fire.

WolfShe rolled out her mat near the grandfather and pretended to sleep. She didn't want to speak to the brave in the corner, much less look at him, or have his gaze upon her. Later, through almost-closed eyes, she saw Running Bear propped up against the cedar wall, head tipped forward, snoring lightly like a puppy. She smelled his scent, now milder, a mixture of pine sap and cedar boughs. He smelled good, she assumed because of the medicines.

First light, pale as a seashell on this gray, cold day, creeped into the longhouse. Running Bear jumped up when his grandfather shouted, "Running Bear, where's my bow?"

"Grandfather? Your bow? Outside. I'll get it."

Running Bear stepped around WolfShe as she pressed a hot drink to grandfather's lips, stumbled past the medicine baskets, and ran outside in the freezing drizzle to fetch the bow and arrows from the drying hut. He returned and handed them to his grandfather, but the old man refused with a wave of his hand and demanded, "Give them to the medicine woman who healed me, Running Bear." Running

Bear approached WolfShe, just close enough to hand the bow and arrows over. She accepted them without looking at him. "Yours," grandfather said, a faint gurgle swimming with his words.

WolfShe didn't know what to do. Bow and arrows were precious, a gift for a boy—not just a boy—the favorite son. She knew she couldn't refuse the giver, or the gift. Why would he give this to me? she wondered. Why not to his grandson?

"Honorable One, I don't hunt. I gather. I know nothing of a bow."

"You have a knife. Why not a bow? You may use it some-day…you may need it. My gift. You brought wind into my chest again."

WolfShe smiled at the old man. "You are generous and kind. Thank you for the honor. I don't expect payment for my work. I do my duty as medicine woman."

"I know, child. I'm no stranger to you, or you to me. I had seen you before…when you were very young. I saw something in you then that now burns like a fire."

"Honorable One?" WolfShe said, dreading what he meant.

Ama stepped inside the drape, smiled when she saw him upright, and said to the old man, "Yes, I remember. You visited. My girl hid behind the baskets. I didn't think you saw her."

"I did. Remember, I asked about her parents. Disap-peared in the Great Flood, you said. I asked about her tribal tongue. She didn't have words. She couldn't capture them, you said, so you taught her ours."

"Yes. She grunted, squeaked, growled, and hissed at you from behind the baskets. I remember now."

"But I saw something that day I never mentioned, the glow in her eyes like a night animal's. Seeing her again, I recognize what that is. She has Far North Clan in her. I've heard tales of their wildness. You see it in their eyes. They glow. She reminds me of…"

"Of what?" WolfShe blurted out. "Do I look like someone you know?"

Ama shot her a look. The old man studied WolfShe's face and slumped back, gasping. "Don't strain. Rest," Ama said and motioned for WolfShe to rub his back again.

WolfShe whispered, "Honorable One. I will rub heating salve into your chest. Then you will sleep again…and heal. But when you wake, promise to tell me more."

The old man said, "Find who you are, find your people. They wait for you." His eyes, fixed on a distant point, closed. He slept.

WolfShe thought Running Bear's eyes misted, but she couldn't be sure in the dim light. Maybe it was hers? She felt overwhelmed with sadness and longing for her family. The mention of them pierced her heart. She shifted her attention, so she wouldn't cry.

Running Bear looked like a young elk buck, gangly but strong, wild yet fiercely protective of his family. She liked that. She hadn't noticed it before. She wondered at his angular face. Did it hold knowledge? Something she couldn't define came over her. She threw her wild, jumbled thoughts away and focused on her work. Closing her eyes, she leaned against the elder's chest and heard a swoosh of air. "Good. The sea leaves him. Hot broth, salve rubs, warmth—these will cure him," she said to Running Bear as he eased his grandfather down on the sleeping mat and covered him with his favorite woodpecker-feather and dog-hair blanket.

CHAPTER FOUR

Justice Wolf

Two days later, Ama and WolfShe departed, confident the elder was over the worst of wet lung, leaving ample herbs and instructions for healing broths. Running Bear rushed up when he noticed they had put their medicine baskets outside.

"I will walk you home."

"No need, son," Ama replied. "We know our way, and the day is clear. We stop to visit along the way. Take care of your grandfather. He heals with every sunrise, but true strength returns slowly."

WolfShe felt relieved Ama hadn't accepted the offer. She wanted to talk to her on the journey, something she wouldn't do if Running Bear could hear. She pulled her shawl close around her head and shoulders but saw Running Bear whisper something in Ama's ear. Ama smiled. She tipped her head and said goodbye to him and his family.

When they had walked beyond the village, WolfShe said, "Ama, what did he say to you?"

Ama smiled. "He thanked us. He said he brings firewood for us soon."

"You said *no*, didn't you?"

"Why would I?"

"I collect our wood. We don't need his help."

"Child, when a gift is given, don't refuse. Remember that. Great Spirit wants us to give and to get. As medicine woman, many gifts will come to you. Accept them, like you did the bow and arrows. The circle of healing means you get in return, at some time and in some way, for your healing service. Would you refuse a gift of kindness? Would you refuse to treat someone? If a healer chooses who to help, who is worthy, who is not, then her powers dissolve. They are there, like salt in seawater, but they can't be fully used. Treat all in need. Allow those you serve to complete the circle. Great Spirit respects Earth Mother, Sister Moon, Brother Sun, and every creature in and under the sky and sea. Our Creator's way is our way. Do not shun a gift WolfShe…of any kind."

"Yes, Ama," WolfShe said, running her tongue over the seam in her lower lip, "extra firewood will be good, gives me more time to gather herbs."

"When Running Bear brings firewood, we thank and feed him. His grandfather gave you a bow and arrow out of respect, an unusual gift for a girl. You are hard on Running Bear. He was a good boy and now a better man. I regret I haven't taken you out more. You don't know how to act. From now on, we will travel more, after winter. You are good with the ill, but the healthy?"

WolfShe didn't reply. Ama's words made her feel as if she'd been spotted naked, bathing in a stream. She wanted to live as they were, just the two of them. WolfShe closed her eyes to send her wish to the sky. But something interfered. She realized she could smell Running Bear's scent from a great distance—woodsmoke, herbs, and something she couldn't recognize. She smiled, thinking he'd be easy to track.

They hadn't gone far before Running Bear trotted up behind, breathing hard. "Medicine Woman Ama, a messenger came for you. Your aunt asks that you come to her."

Ama considered the request and said to WolfShe, "We'll stay the night with her and leave early tomorrow."

"Ama. I can walk home alone."

"No. My people want to know you better. We're getting old. You must remember us. We will be your ancestors."

"Ama, let me go home by myself. I'm a tracker. You said you've never seen anyone with my skills, remember?"

"Yes, girl. I remember. I taught you everything you know."

WolfShe hung her head. She hadn't meant to challenge Ama, especially in front of a smelly boy. "Yes, Ama."

"Thank you, Running Bear. You are welcome anytime at our cabin. Let us know how your grandfather heals."

Running Bear tipped his head *yes* and ran back in the direction he'd come from, without looking at WolfShe.

"You are not kind to that boy. You could have greeted him. He could keep you safe."

"From what?"

"From yourself, from your lack of understanding. Not all Two-Leggeds are good like Running Bear's family. There are men who would take you."

"Where?"

"Girl! For pleasure. Not our people…but others. You know nothing of mating. You will learn when you marry."

"Mating? I do know things. I know I have no longing for that. I see animals in the meadow, especially Elk People, mating. No, I do not want that."

"Those are Four-Leggeds. Man's love, well, at some point you will want it. I was like you at your age. Wait for kindness, girl. Wait for your heart to tell you. Then you will be happy with your choice of mate."

"Were you happy with yours, Ama?"

"Yes, for a lifetime. He was kind and good."

"I don't need a mate. I don't want one. I can do everything a man can do, better."

"Grow up. Then decide. Some medicine women don't take mates. Taking care of others is a full life's work. Maybe a mate would help, but maybe not. A boy like Running Bear would. Since my aunt sent for me, she has something to say. You can leave at first light if I stay longer."

⁂

WolfShe looked forward to setting out early, alone. She collected her medicine baskets, empty of medicines but overflowing with gifts. She put them in the corner by the entrance. She thought about Ama's aunt, how she had welcomed her and complimented her dark hair and eyes, *full of power*, she said, *just like Ama's people.* WolfShe thought it strange the old aunt seemed to think since Ama had raised her, she somehow had Ama's family blood running in her. The aunt gave WolfShe a parting gift, an eagle feather, saying *it's a special gift to protect you from harm.*

She accepted me. I do belong to Ama's family. WolfShe felt warmth spread across her like sun sweeping meadow grass. We are blessed to have you in our family, the aunt had said. WolfShe wondered, Would Ama's aunt welcome me if I told her about Black Snake, the evil one that lives in darkness, swims in an ebony pond, and curses me with horrible visions to render me weak, so he can feed on my power?

WolfShe looked at the others asleep in the dull warmth of last night's embers and silently pulled on her elk hide boots, shawl, and hat. She secured the knife to her waist and stepped out with her baskets, not waking anyone, a talent she attributed to living alone in the woods as a child.

The morning red-tinged clouds shrouded the distant mountaintops. Mist the color of salmon hung low in the forest. She couldn't recall such light. A fierce sea wind carried disturbed shrieks of gulls. Ravens flew deep into the forest for safety, their black wings slicing in-and-out of the sick mist like knives. An ill wind slapped WolfShe in the face with a menacing hand. She pulled her shawl close, feeling glad Ama had stayed behind. She tucked her head and trotted into the unnatural wind.

WolfShe skirted the forest, following the tree line as far as she could, keeping the meadow to her right. When she caught glimpses of the sea, the gray churning waves appeared confused, unclear which direction to come ashore, crashing into each other, ripping down the shore. She decided at the far end of the forest, she would take the rocky path over the hill and down to the meadow to follow the stream home. Longer but safer.

Her mind drifted back to Running Bear's sick grandfather. She wondered how he fared. She had not liked staying in their longhouse with so many people, especially with Running Bear. He made her uncomfortable. How could Ama expect *her* to sleep with him so near? He had no problem sleeping, even though he smelled. She laughed and shouted to the trees. "I smell like herbs and ointments…but Running Bear? Wild danger and honey."

WolfShe pulled up short. She heard a sound overhead in the cedar boughs. A twig snapped. She saw nothing. She veered further into the woods. Low to the ground, grayed pink vapor swirled over decaying logs and settled on delicate sword ferns. WolfShe stood still, listening. She heard breathing…not hers. Her body tightened. She lowered her baskets without a sound, withdrew her knife from its sheath, and scanned the forest, tilting her head side to side to listen. Through the heavy mist, she sensed movement.

"Who's there? Show yourself," she shouted. No answer. Her back tightened. Her leg muscles tensed to run. She had never used her knife on a human. She wasn't sure she could.

A dark silhouette moved. She shouted, "Wolf?" Dark fur became visible like a demon in a dream; the animal faltered. He lowered his head and sniffed the ground. His snout lifted. His gums pulled back over long white fangs. He growled. The sound hit her stomach like a rock.

"Will you eat me now for saving you? I had to cut off that paw." The wolf seemed stunned. He stared without moving. WolfShe studied him—the largest, darkest charcoal wolf she'd ever seen. She feared this could be another. Swirling mist erased his legs. "Let me step back to the meadow, Brother Wolf. This forest is yours. I will not harm you."

The wolf lunged toward her, landing so close he could have bitten her, but he backed away and trotted off into the mist. She remained frozen, knife-in-hand. The wolf traced a half-circle in the trees and returned.

"Wolf Brother, creature…or spirit?" The animal gazed up at her, his golden eyes penetrating and still. The mist parted. She saw he balanced on three legs. She touched his fur. The thick mantle of neck fur, soft and damp, reassured her. "Creature of the earth. My friend. You scared me."

   Dyan Dubois

She stroked the length of his spine. She smelled the air fill with his scent—musky earth, cedar, sword fern, and silver rain—the same scent that had lingered on her hands after she released him from the trap but sweet, untinged with blood, pain, and fear.

She heard a howl. Wolf's ears flicked forward. With tail raised, he bolted upland. WolfShe watched him disappear in the trees and mist, wishing she could run with him. She decided to backtrack to the meadow rather than take the shortcut through the woods. She wasn't scared of her wolf… but the pack was hunting.

She descended the rocky path to the meadow. Ground fog swirled through sleeping grasses like pale spirits. WolfShe spotted a person running in the distance. The sound of his feet pounding the earth, his arched shoulders, his chin tipped upward, the long braids slapping side to side, told her: Running Bear. She was happy to recognize him. She caught his scent…with pleasure. He turned her direction. Running at me? Stupid boy! She snarled and stamped the ground. Anger flared in her like a burning branch, rising higher and higher. She clenched her teeth.

Running Bear shouted: "WolfShe!"

"Why do you run in this mist? Is Ama safe?"

"To collect wood for you. Where's Ama? You're alone? I could have traveled with you."

"She stayed with her aunt," WolfShe said, trying to sound calm. "How is your grandfather?"

"He breathes well. His chest doesn't sound like the sea. He eats well."

"Good. I must go."

"Then we walk together."

"Try to keep up."

WolfShe darted along the deer path through the meadow. She acted like she couldn't hear Running Bear, until he bellowed, "Let me carry your baskets." She stopped and handed him one, the lightest. Running Bear smiled and strapped it on his back. WolfShe took off at a run. He took off at a run, keeping pace beside her. She slowed to a walk when they neared the first village. He slowed with her. Where the path narrowed, Running Bear stepped in front of her to go first along the slippery rocks by the waterfall. Irritated, WolfShe followed. They moved slowly on the trail. Icy mist covered the rocks. Her medicine basket slid sideways, throwing her off-balance. Running Bear reached out to grab her hand. She glanced down at their locked hands. His palm like golden elk leather warmed by a fire made her furious. She yanked her hand away and took off again.

Near a village, Running Bear halted abruptly. "My cousin will have her first baby soon. Could you see her, make sure she is well?"

"I need to get home."

"Medicine Woman?"

WolfShe knew her duty and nodded *yes*. When she saw a woman standing at a longhouse entrance, yelling and waving them over, WolfShe grew concerned. "Who is her birthing helper, Running Bear?" Then she heard, "Come celebrate our girl baby!"

"She doesn't need my help. The baby has come. I must go."

Running Bear's aunt ran to embrace him and greet his companion. "Take food with us, celebrate. Medicine Woman of Wolf Totem? You've come. How did you know? Both mother and baby are healthy. Grandfather also, he's shouting orders. He praises Medicine Woman of Wolf Totem."

"Grandfather made the journey? He is very ill," Running

     D Y A N D U B O I S

Bear said and looked at WolfShe.

When WolfShe walked in, chatter stopped. The family stood and stared. She clenched her hands in front of her, gripping her basket leathers until her fingers went pale. From the far corner of the longhouse, she heard her name bounce along the wooden planks.

Running Bear's grandfather, wrapped in blankets, motioned her over. "Medicine Woman, you came without being called. You knew. Just like you knew wind would enter my chest again. I breathe with no pain. I commanded my family to carry me here to see our new baby."

WolfShe glanced at Running Bear. "He shouldn't go out in damp cold."

"You chased the evil spirits away, beat them out of me, you and that wolf of yours. Come see our new baby, I hope for many more. My Running Bear," he said putting his hand on Running Bear's shoulder, "is a fine brave. He would make a good mate for you."

WolfShe felt eyes weigh her down like boulders. She replied quickly, "Let me listen to you." She placed her ear on his chest. "Deep breath. Another. Another." She looked up. "Rumbling down deep gurgles like an underground spring. You rest." She pulled the last herb packets from her basket and handed them to him. "Steep in hot water until the water looks like mud. Pick out floating roots and leaves. Drink warm four times during daylight. And before sleep, this one in water," she said and handed him a small pouch of fine powder. "Two pinches at night, no more." WolfShe tapped his spine up and down with her fist and wrapped the blanket around him. Lie down and rest."

"You have strong hands, girl, capable hands. You must be a good weaver."

"Honorable One, I weave only in winter when I cannot be outside. I do all the work at home. I am very strong. I bring in wood, make ropes, prepare medicines, harvest plants, beat cedar bark into cloth, carve, weave, everything… for Ama and me. I will take care of us…always."

"Someday you will want company. Think of our long-house as yours. Visit us. We are family. The Great Flood changed many lives, girl. I'm happy to see how strong and quick you are, in mind and body. Ama took good care of you. She taught you her wisdom. People talk about you… and that wolf. From *metul* teeth pale men use, you cut him free. Wolf lives as a Three-Legged. Did Ama tell you that she asked Running Bear to watch your cabin when she saw a lame wolf haunting her woods. She feared a spirit demon, posing as a wolf, wanted to lure you away."

WolfShe felt like a rabbit in a meadow with red-tailed hawks flying overhead. "You've seen Three-Legged? Do you think him spirit demon, or living wolf?"

"Living wolf. Ama tested Running Bear with that request. One night she thought you'd seen Running Bear because you talked of a moving shadow in the trees. Ama is very fond of my grandson, ever since she helped birth him. She saved him. The birthing cord choked him. He's like her son. And you are a daughter to me. Sit with us before you go. I want to tell you something about your Ama, from the time before she found you. Did you know Ama's famous for stories; she entertained at potlatches for many years. One of her best stories, about a *Justice Wolf,* she quit telling after she found you. I will tell you her story."

"If you drink your medicine slowly. I'll stay and listen, Honorable One," WolfShe said as the family gathered around the firepit.

Long, long ago Great Spirit created fish of the waters, animals of the land, birds of the sky, trees, plants, all life, fliers, crawlers, clingers, everyone. Yet Great Spirit wanted something more, so Two-Leggeds came into being. Everyone and everything lived in harmony. Earth Mother cared for her children, protected, and provided for them. But as time went on, Great Spirit asked Raven to assign respected wolves to report on human progress. You see, in The Long Ago wolves and humans did not fear each other. Great Spirit favored wolves, allowing them to walk upright on two legs, so they could see farther if they wanted.

Raven worried. He felt of all creation, humans lacked understanding, but he felt choosing wolves unusual, so he mustered his courage and asked Great Spirit: "Why wolves?" The answer—they see from a better angle and move fast—disappointed Raven. "But surely ravens are faster and smarter?" Raven replied. Great Spirit smiled and said, "Raven, you question my wisdom? The truth is—your people gossip. Choose the most noble wolves for this service. They will be called the League of Justice Wolves and will report to you, and you to me."

One day a Justice Wolf reported to Raven that he had come upon a group of humans on the beach, fighting over who caught which fish and how they would divide the day's catch. The wolf had never seen such shouting and hitting. What happened next alarmed him. The male human on the ground yelled that he didn't believe in Great Spirit, and he didn't believe humans must share food. The one who catches the fish, eats the fish, he said. Everyone must find their own.

Raven clucked and stamped his feet in revulsion and reported to Great Spirit that something in creation had gone very wrong with humans. Great Spirit ordered the League of Justice Wolves to monitor human behavior. Justice Wolves traveled, spoke to many tribes, helped solve their problems, and reported to Raven.

One day—ages later—a Justice Wolf named Standing Wolf spotted a young woman picking salmonberries. He walked up to her, upright on two legs. She had never seen such a thing. She was very scared.

The wolf spoke to her in the young woman's native tongue. She was horrified and surprised a wolf could talk. She started to run, but her feet froze like ice. Standing Wolf promised her he would not hurt her. He settled down on the ground next to her, saying he wanted only to talk. His duty, assigned by Great Spirit, he recounted, was to find out how humans got along and to help them solve their problems.

He asked about her village, how her people lived, what they ate, how they treated creatures of the land and sea but most importantly how they treated each other. He was pleased with her descriptions of village life by the river. When he stood and stretched to a great height on two legs, the woman cowered. He settled down on his haunches, wrapping his bushy tail close to his flanks and relaxed. They promised to meet at the patch every day of picking season to talk about human life.

Standing Wolf spoke in a voice—soft but deep—to the young woman who, putting her berry basket aside, sat down to relax and listen. Standing Wolf asked her to meet him every day at the salmonberry patch, and he would tell her a new story. They met often, and with every visit, they grew more comfortable with each other. They laughed, talked, and smiled.

One day Standing Wolf didn't appear. The young woman felt a deep pain in her heart. She had grown fond of his stories and the time they spent together. She continued to walk to the patch to look for the wolf, but he didn't come. On the last day of berry season, Standing Wolf returned. He walked up, towering above her, and looked down at the sadness in her eyes. Standing Wolf felt the same sadness. The girl confessed she had missed him, that she had fallen in love with him, and her heart broke when he went away.

Standing Wolf reported her words to Raven. Upon hearing this, Great Spirit bellowed: "Beings must pair with their own kind, duck-to-duck, swan-to-swan, wolf-to-wolf, human to human. That is my Creative Design. Have Standing Wolf come to me at once!"

Raven raced across the sky to deliver the message. Hearing the command, Standing Wolf charged up Spirit Mountain on all fours. He reached High Clouds Silver Bridge and jumped through night stars to run beyond the moon. He called out: "Great Spirit, hear me." The sky rumbled and cracked. Great Spirit shouted: "Tell me, Standing Wolf, why human love? I granted wolf-kind gifts of upright walk, the eyes to see far, and the ability to settle disputes. That was enough."

Standing Wolf answered, "Great Spirit the human girl loves me, and I love her. You created us. This is your fault."

Great Spirit cracked the lower sky. Clouds rumbled and collided; jagged white lightning bombarded Standing Wolf. He danced upright, sidestepping the spears. Water poured from the sky and washed him down Spirit Mountain. He crouched on all fours.

Great Spirit shouted, "You, Standing Wolf, are clever. You watched human creatures. You learned their ways. Your cunning is your undoing. I gave you speed, intelligence, strength, the ability to walk upright, but I did not make you human! You disappointed me. From now on, you must speak your own tongue to your own kind, four paws on the ground. Humans will fear you. They will flee at the sight of you."

"Forgive me, Great Spirit, I hang my head in grief. I disappointed you…and myself. Punish me but not my kind. Let Justice Wolves continue. Please, do not punish the human woman. She has done nothing wrong. Fling me against the highest mountain. Drop me into the lowest ravine. Bury me in the ocean. Let this end with me, but do not end my kind."

"Remorse, Standing Wolf? I instilled that trait in humans, not wolves. Your association with the woman has shaped you, touched you with human spirit. I did not intend this. From now on, wolves will live in dens in the ground, away from humans. You are the last Justice Wolf. I will allow no more."

"Great Spirit. I honor your decision. I beg your forgiveness. I meant no harm. I accept your ruling, but I ask for mercy for wolves. Do not punish all Justice Wolves because of me."

Great Spirit softened. He replied, "I will not stop Wolf People from sharing the earth with humans. Standing Wolf, because you accepted your fate with dignity, I grant you this boon. From ancient times when Great Whale chose wolf-life to save a human girl, wolves have been special to me. I decree I will grant a few very special wolves the ability to communicate their respect for humans. In return, certain humans will protect your people from harm in order to honor Great Whale's legacy."

⸺◦◦◦⸺

GRANDFATHER STOPPED AND CLEARED HIS THROAT. "Ama always ended her story saying Great Spirit allowed a few special wolves to carry on the work of Justice Wolves. They serve human healers when the need is great. But be warned children: Avoid wolves. You can't tell if a wolf is a Justice Wolf by the way it looks. Never go near any wolf. Remember this rhyme: *Always stay near your mother when you play, in case a wolf passes your way.* She also taught the children you can tell evil by the way it smells. Think of rotting salmon and skunk spray. Evil catches in your throat and makes your stomach jump. When you smell something like that, run home as fast as the wind. And don't go wandering alone, especially when it's getting dark. Evil moves quickly in the dark."

The old man looked at WolfShe sitting stone-still with dew on her cheeks. He whispered, "Warming salve makes my eyes water too. Go wash your hands, eat, and Running Bear will see you home. The woods are full of wolves these days. You wouldn't want to stumble onto one. Would you?"

"Why did Ama not tell this story to me?"

"Because of you. She stopped telling that story when she found you."

⸺◦◦◦⸺

ON THE TRAIL HOME WOLFSHE SAID NOTHING. RUNNING Bear spoke, but his words died, unnoticed. WolfShe walked twice as fast as his long strides to stay ahead of him. When she slowed, Running Bear tried again.

"Do you like the bow and arrows Grandfather gave you?"

"Haven't tried them. I don't kill things."

"How do you live?" Running Bear said, smiling at her. "No wonder you're so small."

WolfShe's ears burned. Bitterness puckered her mouth like unripe berries.

"Makes me fast. Tall people like you fall more, tangle easier, break easier."

"I stumbled when I grew a hand's length in two seasons…but not now. I'm steady in body, heart, and mind." He smiled at WolfShe. She looked away. "I like walking with you."

WolfShe could think of no reply, thinking, Running Bear admitted he was clumsy. I would never. What's wrong with him? No brave admits a lack of balance and strength.

When Ama greeted them at the cabin door, WolfShe was surprised to see her.

"How is your grandfather, Running Bear?"

"Good, Ama. WolfShe treated him at my aunt's house. My cousin birthed her baby, a girl."

Ama stared at WolfShe. WolfShe knew Ama saw the smoldering fire in her face. "Many blessings. Come in, drink hot broth," Ama raised her eyebrows at WolfShe, "before you journey home…or stay the night here."

WolfShe's eyes flared at Ama's offer. In our cabin? she thought. No! She looked away so neither Running Bear nor Ama could see the red anger scorching her face.

"Thank you, Ama, I return to my cousin's."

WolfShe looked at Ama. Deep creases flowed across her brow like a muddy river; her lips pulled tight. "Ama, Running Bear attends to his grandfather. We will see his family at the next potlatch."

Ama stepped inside to grab a feather blanket she had made for the baby. "Here, for the new baby, and honeycomb for the mother to make her strong."

WolfShe walked into the cabin, pulled the drape to her corner, and left them standing at the cabin entrance.

"I will come in two sunrises to collect firewood for you." His voice dropped. "Grandfather wanted me to tell you, Ama, a Pale Face was spotted in the east upland forest burying *metul* teeth traps. He strips the animal's pelt and leaves the body to rot. He's the same one who trapped Three-Legged."

WolfShe popped out from behind her curtain to see Ama's lip quivering.

"You must hurry, Running Bear, night comes soon," Ama said and waved him off, pulling the plank door shut.

"Ama, I heard. Don't worry. We're safe."

"Girl, you need to treat people as well as you treat animals…as well as you treat that wolf."

"I would if Running Bear was injured."

Ama stared hard at WolfShe, one eyebrow cocked like a mountain peak. "You had a Three-Legged visitor. He was curled in front of our door when I arrived. I've never had a wolf at my door. I don't like it. Could be he's flesh-wolf, or spirit-wolf. Wolves are very clever. They can change."

"He's flesh. I saw him on my walk home. He's not spirit. His charcoal fur was damp with strands of moonlight woven in. He smells sweet."

"Then?"

"He loped away when Running Bear appeared."

"Did the wolf and Running Bear see one another?"

"No."

"Are you sure, girl?" Ama said, visibly shaking. WolfShe wrapped her arm around the old woman's shoulders.

"Why?"

"I have a hunch about that wolf. Be careful, girl. Don't go alone into the forest. Running Bear's message…the pale-faced trapper, he's out there and he wants that wolf…and you. Obey me. The wolf and the trapper do a dangerous dance with you in the middle. Hear me, girl? Give your oath. Do not go into the forest alone! The wolf lures the trapper; the trapper slays the wolf. Death comes to anyone in-between."

WolfShe's heart burned seeing Ama's fear. Ama had grown old and weak. She's not the Medicine Woman of Raven Totem who adopted me, the bravest, strongest woman I knew. She needs protection.

CHAPTER FIVE

Intruder

Two months of freezing rain kept Ama and WolfShe close to their cabin. WolfShe enjoyed the long dark, but Ama's years weighed on her. They wouldn't always have time to sit by the fire, share stories, weave, and make herbal medicines, WolfShe realized. Her own mother, far away in the Land of Mists, had become a curl of woodsmoke, a vapor, a flicker that sparked and drifted upward through the hole in their cedar roof. The more WolfShe tried to see, the harder it became. She imagined her mother dressed in Ama's clothes, speaking Ama's words. She longed to keep the memory of her mother from slipping through her fingers.

WolfShe sat by the firepit pulling cedar fibers to beat into bandages. She thought about Running Bear's grandfather, cured of wet lung, but illness comes quickly to old people, especially in the chill of winter. Ama could be next.

"Ama, I've been thinking of something we should have ready if wet lung spreads wide this winter. Medicine mats."

"What? Never heard of them," Ama said, stirring the soup.

"Yes, you have. I got the idea from you. You taught me herb craft, but I've thought of a way to help, even if we can't reach the ill person. We make medicine mats. We'll take them to longhouses and explain how and when to use them. We'll weave chest-cure herbs into small cedar mats. If someone falls ill, a family member can slather on clear-breath salve, dampen the medicine mat, place it over the salve, wrap the person in blankets with hot rocks at their feet, and let them sweat out the illness. What do you think, Ama?"

Ama looked at WolfShe, the firelight dancing in her eyes. "Very good, Medicine Woman. You go beyond my teaching. Great Spirit smiles on you. I'll weave the mats. You prepare the herbs. We'll put the salve into folded reed packets and take your medicine mats to winter potlaches to hand out. But barter for what you need, WolfShe. You must think about that."

"What do we need, Ama? We have full stores of food, medicines, clothes. Maybe something special?"

"Like?"

"A bracelet, or an abalone shell necklace?"

"Body decoration? You've never cared before."

"I like colors, Ama. Abalone shells look like sea, sky, and mountains all swirled into one. Is that bad?"

"No, but I think I should stop calling you *girl* now. You have a young woman's desire…to look beautiful."

WolfShe felt heat rise in her cheeks. "No, Ama. I have seen my reflection in still water. I am not beautiful. But I love shells and colors."

"Make a medicine mat. Let me see what is offered," Ama said with a smile. "We will announce at Long Night Potlatch each family can have one. No one will take without giving in return. Accept what is given, WolfShe, whatever it is. That night, I step down as Medicine Woman. You step up."

"I'm not ready, Ama. I don't have wisdom. No one will listen to me. No one can replace you. They won't trust me because I don't know my ancestral totem. It may not be Wolf, as you think."

"They will listen. My word goes a long way. You have seen fifteen summers. You have studied with me for ten. Yes, you are young, but many know of your skills. Running Bear's grandfather speaks of you far and wide. I will declare you—blessed by me, taught by me—the best choice to take on my duties as medicine woman. I look now toward life's sunset. I must prepare for that journey. You, as my adopted daughter, can work under my totem. I will guide you from the Land of Mists."

"Ama, you are Medicine Woman of Raven Totem and will be for many winters. You know ravens don't speak to me. How can they guide my healing hands if I can't understand them? I understand you, no one else."

"Daughter. You don't listen. Your ears are filled with whispering wind. Assume my duties. Let the tribes believe in whichever totem, Wolf or Raven. The rest will fall into place."

WolfShe glowed at Ama calling her *Daughter.* But to think of Ama in her twilight hung like a heavy stone around her neck. To think of Ama guiding her from the Land of Mists with Raven Totem alarmed her. WolfShe would be vulnerable during the three-day transition after Ama left her body. Would Black Snake strike? With no ancestors rallied around her, could she repel his evil? Who would shield her? She did not ask Ama. The stone around her neck sunk deeper. She had no totem. Her ancestors were lost to her. She couldn't call on them, be guided by them, receive blessings from them. She had no one to claim her from the other side. She realized she must face life alone.

Ravens didn't speak to her, protect her. Ama hoped they would, but they didn't. A lone wolf saved from a trap does not make an ancestor's pledge, she knew. The only clear sign, the one that wouldn't leave, Black Snake, whispered to her in dreams. He commanded her to look upon him—her totem—and do his bidding. He slithered in the black pond, opened wide his fangs, and threatened to devour her beloved Ama if she didn't obey. WolfShe would wake in a sweat, shaking with fear and run to check on Ama sleeping peacefully on her mat. WolfShe knew she must be stronger. She must defeat Black Snake before Ama transitions. She had to journey to that underground pool and poison him. But how?

Ama smiled at her. "WolfShe, you are no longer a child…a girl. You've grown into a powerful young woman. The name I gave you when I found you unsettles me now."

"WolfShe makes you uneasy?"

"Yes. The name, not a power name, began as an imagining. You were thin and small, half-starved. How you survived in the wild, alone, I could only imagine. So, I did imagine. Remember me saying I thought wolves suckled you?"

"Yes, Ama. You grinned."

"I no longer grin, Daughter. I wonder. No human child could have lived through the Great Flood, been tossed into the mountain forest, and survived…without help. Most likely wolves would have found you, but they would have eaten you. Can you remember anything from that time?"

WolfShe sat quietly gazing at the flames rising and falling with drafts. She felt her face harden, her jaw clench, her brows stitch tight like moccasin leathers. She exhaled and closed her eyes.

"Yes, small visions drift by, memories of clouds overhead. Running elk. Water dropping from rocks. Strong winds. Slapping trees. Bright green moss. Vomiting bitter mushrooms. Sky falling, earth cracking. Blue sea." WolfShe leaned forward and grabbed her knees, rocking back and forth, whimpering. Ama moved close, wrapped her arms around WolfShe, and pulled her to her heart.

"Daughter, I'm sorry I asked."

WolfShe whispered, "And a man." Ama gripped her arm to stop WolfShe's rocking. "Spirit white."

Ama wiped back tears. "You never mentioned this before. Spirit or flesh? What did he do?"

"The Black Snake told him where to look for me. I saw him, human but with sky-blue eyes, cedar-red hair on his face and head, and a broken front tooth. His face wavered like smoke; his words sounded like rocks and wood chips rubbed together. I ran on all fours, faster than a rabbit. He disappeared into mist." WolfShe trembled. She crawled onto Ama's lap like a baby. Ama rocked her gently and chanted protection prayers until she fell asleep.

When she woke, WolfShe didn't know how long she had slept, but the fire had dwindled to small embers, and Ama lay asleep on her mat, snoring. WolfShe pulled a blanket over Ama and walked outside to relieve herself in the bushes. She stepped off the creaking entry planks into the crisp night, stars piercing the black sky like silver-pointed arrows. A passing cloud roamed Sacred Mountain but broke apart to expose four bright stars lined up in an arc over the peak. WolfShe wondered if the stars were a walkway to the Land of Spirits, a sign. She couldn't recall seeing them before.

Something moved. Her eyes darted to the tree shadows. She jumped up from a squat. A twig snapped behind her. She heard a breathy whine, jumped away, and whipped around.

"You? You appear without warning, sounding only a whimper? I haven't seen you in moons. Tonight, you step out of shadows. Why?"

Three-Legged hopped closer. WolfShe stood still, scanning the darkness for other movement. Nothing. Not even an owl shifted position. Wolf lowered his head, leaned in, and rubbed against her leg. They stood body to body, warmth to warmth, in silence. WolfShe felt the comfort of wolf's presence. She stroked his thick fur. She felt their spirits join like two streams flowing together to form one river in timeless recognition. Then she patted wolf on the head and walked to the cabin entrance. She knew this wolf would never hurt her. He seemed to owe her, for saving him, she assumed. She stepped into the cabin. Wolf hopped in. She watched him sniff the air, his large, dark head lowered in Ama's direction. He curled his lip slightly and breathed her scent. His gold eyes showed no fear, nor aggression. WolfShe let him stay.

WolfShe loaded dry branches onto the embers. Flames nibbled at the wood and blazed bright. The wolf shied away. WolfShe led him to her sleeping corner and pulled the curtain. When she settled on her mat, pulling a blanket over her, wolf lowered to her side.

<hr>

MORNING LIGHT SNEAKED THROUGH THE CABIN DOOR and tickled WolfShe's lids. She bolted upright, eyes wide. Wolf? She peered around the curtain. Ama stood stoking the fire to heat water.

"Ama, where's wolf?"

"Wake. Leave your dreams. We have work to do."

"Ama, wolf was here with us last night. Did you see him?"

"No wolf can enter my house. A protection prayer lives at the entrance."

WolfShe caught Ama's look, sorrow tinged with fear, and realized she should say no more. "I dreamed."

"Spirit wolves have many tricks, Daughter. Did wolf speak in your dream?"

"No."

"Growl?"

"No."

"Did you first see him in moonlight?"

"Yes."

"Did he smell strong and sickening?"

"No, Ama. He smelled like new ferns, sweet and fresh."

Ama shook her head. "In your dream he was here, inside our cabin, with a fire glowing in the pit?"

"Yes. He curled up next to me. We fell asleep. When I woke, he was gone."

"Naturally. How can a dream continue when you wake? Spirit Wolves don't fear fire like real wolves. Sweet smell? Great Spirit sent you a kindred-spirit dream. It's a sign. Great Spirit tells you Wolf is your totem, just as I thought from the way you survived, and then you saved a real wolf's life. Kindred spirits are always welcome in my house. Evil cannot enter where Great Spirit sends kindred spirits."

"Yes, kindred spirit," WolfShe repeated. "So, you would welcome wolf in our house?"

"More than welcome, Daughter. That kindred spirit wolf is a blessing. I open our door to him."

WolfShe began to doubt her memory. She knew a real wolf could not have stayed. Yet she had felt his fur, heard his breath. She wondered, what kind of test could this be? Wolf must be a tempter. Her stomach cinched and turned cold like meadow frost. Black Snake? Could he do this? He wants to lure me, render me useless, draw me down into his black pit. How better than lure me with the one I saved? She scrubbed her shawl across her heart six times repeating: "Be brave, WolfShe. Do not drink dark thoughts that weaken you. Like phantoms they dry up and turn to dust in daylight."

Since WolfShe's coming-of-age ceremony, she realized many things had happened, some understandable, others not. Dreams and memories, like tangled fishnets, haunted her. In one, her mother told her she had traveled to the Land of Mists after a winter illness. In another, her baby sister played at her side then turned to dust while holding WolfShe's hand. She heard her father shout—she thought calling her—but she couldn't see him. These torments made WolfShe decide Great Spirit rejected her by not taking her with her family to punish her, something she would never express to Ama. She decided the Land of Mists where departed family spirits become revered ancestors was not meant for her. Why else would her family, ushered by the sea, leave her alone—with no totem and no ancestors to work on her behalf? She'd been abandoned because she wasn't good enough to join them.

She felt stuck, not here, not there. Her adopted people couldn't intervene on her behalf. Ama couldn't give her Raven Totem. No ancestor would know where in the mists to look for her when she died, or in which part her spirit would rest. Would she forever cry out for family who cannot hear? Would she trudge through darkness and not see? The thought that she wasn't meant for the Land of Mists blanketed her with sorrow. Tears dripped down her cheeks. Breath caught in her throat and kicked like a wild animal.

My parents can't pull me over, she thought. I'm lost to them. No totem will guide my spirit home. Black Snake plots to drag me underground to live in his darkness, his ebony water. No healer will I be, she feared, only an instrument of his evil.

WolfShe locked her fears deep, away from Ama's sight. She burned incense cedar to purify the air. She regretted the girl Ama had trained in healing wisdom had no wisdom. Ama could do nothing to save her. To imagine a wolf lying beside her—near a fire—surely was the work of Black Snake, his way to possess her, render her useless, and weave a net to bind her to his darkness.

⁓◦⁓

RUNNING BEAR STOPPED BY TO SEE THEM, BUT FINDING only the elder, he appeared disappointed, as Ama recounted to WolfShe. She made no comment. She was glad she had been away, overjoyed. She didn't tell Ama how often she avoided Running Bear. Something in his eyes made her uncomfortable. Around him she felt she'd slipped on a tree root, or misstepped when jumping rocks in the stream, which she never did. She had nothing to say to him. He looked at her like a big-eyed fish gulping for air. She would scowl back at him. He'd quickly look away. WolfShe didn't hate him. She was grateful for the concern he showed Ama. She knew he would make a good mate someday… for someone else. She welcomed spring for many reasons but especially for Running Bear's infrequent visits as he prepared for sea fishing.

WolfShe roamed and enjoyed her freedom. Winter's darkness had retracted like lake ice. Tender plant shoots defied the cold and popped through the meadow crust.

Jagged Peak's teeth bit blue sky. More light for foraging medicine plants, more warmth for Ama's bones, more time for me to search for medicine plants, she thought. Over the winter, WolfShe and Ama had made many house visits; their stores, dwindled to a minimum, needed replenishing.

WolfShe had gone alone to treat the ill after Ama fell sick. Red throat had spread throughout the island with spring's chill winds. Many fell ill. Ama rested at the cabin, content to weave and prepare food but insisted on teaching WolfShe the Parting Prayer Ceremony, a blessing to usher the spirit into the Land of Mists, when one of the elders died from red throat. She said to her, "I healed this time, but you will have to say this prayer for me soon." WolfShe knew Ama had spoken the truth she couldn't face. Now, warmer days would mean Ama's strength would return. WolfShe felt great relief.

On her foraging outings, WolfShe could feel Three-Legged as if a cedar rope bound them. He did not haunt her dreams, but he made his presence felt. Days would pass without her seeing him, and then the wolf would appear. WolfShe began a game, calling him with her thoughts. The first time, nothing happened. The second, he appeared at the cabin at dusk. They regarded one another, and he trotted off. She repeated a thought-call days later. He appeared at dusk. After four calls, and four appearances, she knew the wolf understood.

WolfShe realized Three-Legged might have a den, not far from the cabin, although she'd seen no evidence of one, and a family. At night she could hear distant, muffled howls, but when Three-Legged appeared quickly, approaching in silence and departing without snapping a twig, she assumed he must live near. He never begged for food. To WolfShe he was more spirit than flesh, except she could stroke his stiff fur, smell his woodsy scent, and hear him pant when the woodfire was too hot for him. When he shed huge clumps of fur, WolfShe collected what she found snagged on brambles, or sticking to tree bark, to weave into a blanket. Ama saw the basket of charcoal-gray fur and asked where WolfShe had found it. Her reply, snagged in blackberry brambles near the creek, satisfied Ama.

"Anyone could have found it," Ama said, "but you had luck. That shows Wolf Totem honors you." Ama promised to weave the fur into a totem charm for WolfShe.

"Ama, I've decided I am not Wolf Totem. My people are gone. They never told me our totem…not that I remember. You decided I am Wolf Totem, but you have no reason to believe that. You decided I survived because a wolf raised me. That could not have happened. That's just a story."

"That wolf you healed; this is his fur. I'm sure of it. Dark, almost black, rare for any wolf."

WolfShe didn't want to speak an untruth to Ama…nor did she want to speak the truth. The truth would scare her too much. "I agree, yes, this is his fur, Ama. I am lucky I found it first. Weave it into a blanket for yourself, so you stay warm in winter."

"Warm, yes. Sacred, yes. Powerful, yes. But wolves have another trait, Daughter. They can be sly, just like their cousin coyote. Wolf Totem means large challenges, large rewards…but not an easy life. Choose with care the steps you take. Since you don't know the totem your people carried, use another. Use mine…Raven. Ravens are smart, swift, and have lighter hearts than wolves…and broader vision. Your work, your life would be easier. You could be happy. I am sure Great Spirit would grant you their use."

WolfShe woke abruptly. A floorboard creaked at the cabin entrance. She grabbed her knife. She had set newly greased baskets by the fire to cure. Night roamers smelled the fat, she assumed. She stood in front of sleeping Ama, knife ready.

WolfShe smelled something foul. Not my wolf. Something rotten, she thought. Her heart raced. Her throat tightened. She gulped like swallowing a rock. A loud shriek ripped the night. Hoot owls screeched. A deep, menacing growl pricked her neck like sharp pine needles. She lowered the knife and grabbed the bow and arrows by the entrance. She positioned an arrow, pulled the gut string tight, aimed at the entrance, and waited.

She heard gnashing, growling, tearing…then a horrifying sound, a human shriek. She kicked the entrance boards aside and pointed into the darkness. Ama jumped up and stood behind WolfShe, holding a knife. Ama whispered, "Do what you must." WolfShe shot in the direction of the foul smell. They heard a loud gasp and groan followed by yelps. She loaded again and took aim in the darkness. The arrow zinged through the chilly night air. WolfShe stood at strained attention, head cranked sideways, listening. She heard the arrow thwack a tree. Another howl churned the night. WolfShe loaded and pulled back, poised to shoot, listening.

"WolfShe, was that human or animal?" Ama whispered.

"Both, I think. Ama step to the far side of the fire."

WolfShe edged out beyond the cabin entrance, back arched, bow steady, gut-string pulled tight. She heard a whimper.

"Wolf? Show yourself." Three-Legged hopped onto the entrance boards, taking form in the feeble firelight like a smoke phantom. WolfShe lowered her bow and patted him. She jerked her hand back from his wet fur. "Blood! Ama, fetch water, salve, a curved needle. Wolf's hurt."

"He may bite you. He's wounded. Give him death lily first."

WolfShe motioned wolf to the fire. He slinked toward her, head lowered. A gash high on his left shoulder revealed the sheath of underlying muscle. "This is no animal wound. A clean slit. Wolf fought a knife. Run the needle through the flame," she ordered, as she smeared death lily paste on his gums.

The wolf slumped down. She stuck a ball of paste under the flap of his gum. She chanted and watched his eyes close. With quick movements, she cleaned the gash, ordered Ama to squeeze the flesh together, threaded the curved-bone needle with gut string and stitched tight loops along the top edge of the muscle, and then stitched the skin closed. Three-Legged twitched and moaned but didn't wake.

"This animal trusts you. Death lily doesn't work that fast…unless it kills. How much did you give him?"

"Deep-sleep dose. I explained to him what I needed to do."

"Spirit wolves don't bleed. Flesh wolves don't understand human words. What is this? Many moons have passed. He hasn't forgotten you saved him. He trusts you with his life. He may have saved ours."

"Yes, Ama. I trust him. He trusts me. Keep pressure here while I prepare devil's-club." Ama pressed the damp leaves over the wound. She watched WolfShe study the animal closely. "Painful heat moves away." WolfShe reapplied a fresh compress. When the leaves cooled, she applied another. She blotted the wound, rubbed willow bark salve on the seam, and administered more death lily paste to his lips. "He will lick when he wakes." She stretched the cedar bandage, several layers thick, around wolf's shoulder and chest and tied the ends. "He won't like this. I'll have to keep him quiet for a couple of days."

"Here…with us?"

"Where else?"

"Yes, you're right. Drag your mat next to him, so he smells you and rests."

"Wolf won't wake until first light. Ama. I have to go out now to track…"

"No! He's dangerous. Let him die out there. If he returns, we'll kill him then."

"Ama! We're medicine women…healers. We don't kill. Do we?"

"If we have to. The trapper," Ama said, looking down at the sleeping animal, "he came to our house. He tried to enter. Your wolf stopped him. That man means evil. He doesn't deserve our help. If he lives, he lives. If he dies, good. Great Spirit will deal with him."

"Ama, you never taught me that."

"Evil brings its own punishment. I would only kill if I had to. I never taught you that. I never thought it necessary."

"I will find him, no matter where he is. None of our people would do this. Better to see who's in our woods, hard to fight what you don't know. He tracked wolf here. Why?"

"He came for you, WolfShe."

"For springing his traps?"

"Does wolf travel with you, help you find the traps?"

WolfShe looked down and rubbed wolf's sleeping head and ears. "No, that's too dangerous. I go alone."

"But wolf follows you, doesn't he? That's why you refused Running Bear to walk with you."

"At times I thought he did. Once I saw him. He doesn't walk at my side. He stays hidden in the distance. But since that night he appeared and slept here, I've seen him often."

"That was no dream. He came to you here, in the flesh?" Ama said, shaking her head slowly side-to-side, clucking her tongue.

"Yes. He slept by the fire. Ama, we share the same spirit."

Ama slumped back on her haunches to steady herself, grasping the mat. "How could that be? Human-girl…or wolf-girl. What are you?"

"Human, Ama, your adopted daughter. I'm your kind, like you. You joked wolves must have saved me after the Great Flood. I think your words carried truth. I do remember a wolf lying close to me. I thought it was a dream. Three-Legged understands me. I can hear him—not howls, not words—but what he says in my heart."

"What does wolf say about this attack?"

"Before his body slowed from death lily, he said he followed Pale Face here."

"To kill him?"

"I don't know. His thoughts melted into medicine fog. Pale Face trapper tracks wolf, wolf follows me, tracker follows us."

"Pack more devil's club around wolf's shoulder. Draw out that Pale Face evil. Wolf must have all his strength…in body and spirit. We need him."

Huge drops from Ama's brown eyes slid down her creased, weathered skin. Sobs rattled in her throat. WolfShe pulled Ama to her and felt Ama's thin body collapse like a river weed buffeted by spring flow. She held her steady.

"We must move into the village," Ama whimpered. She stopped to gulp air. "Pack your things while wolf sleeps. But wolf cannot come. He must live here, wild. No one would understand. They would fear you, call you demon-woman—not medicine woman—the one who controls wolf spirits. We will have a name-changing ceremony for you. You will not be known as WolfShe. I fear in that naming I leveled a curse. I'm sorry, Daughter."

"Ama. I will go, as you command. Three-Legged has a pack. He will stay behind. But first I must heal him. I could not leave him weak."

"Thank you. I will tell the council a Pale Face trapper with cedar-red hair roams our woods. The braves will drive him out. Your wolf will be safe. We will be safe…far from here."

WolfShe smelled Ama's fear, a pungent mix of spruce gum and fish. She knew she must obey, for Ama's sake. Her heart sank seeing the old woman shake and gasp like she had run up a mountain. She pulled Ama upright. Ama swayed on unsteady feet, muttering incantations while WolfShe led her to her mat, eased her down, and covered her with their ceremonial woodpecker-feather blanket, the one blessed by Ama's teacher. Ama had always protected her. Now WolfShe knew she must take charge and protect Ama…and others. WolfShe made sleep tea for Ama, holding the cup while she sipped it. She lowered her to the sleeping mat and fanned cedar sprigs to carry her protection prayers up to Great Spirit.

While wolf and Ama snored, WolfShe gathered her medicines. She stuffed a poultice wrap, pain salve, leaves, death lily, and surgery supplies into her elk-leather bag and secured it to her waist, next to her knife. She pulled on her

   Dyan Dubois

boots and shawl and stepped out into the night. She traveled by moonlight.

At first light, when she returned, her wolf roused. Seeing her, he dug his claws into the floor and hoisted upright on three shaky legs. WolfShe reached out to balance him, but he shied away. She realized she carried Pale Face's scent. Before she could stop him, Three-Legged slipped past the entrance boards and disappeared into the pale dawn. WolfShe wanted to run after him but didn't. She wouldn't trust her smell either if she were the wolf.

CHAPTER SIX

Pale Face

WolfShe decided living in River Bend, the nearest village to their cabin, had advantages. In addition to protection, Ama could visit elder women and sit around the firepit telling stories as she weaved. WolfShe enjoyed hearing the stories she'd grown up with. One night, Ama told a story WolfShe had never heard before about the sea sucking down whole islands, spitting up fish, and tossing a whale into the mountain forest. Ama called the story *Whale-Wolf.*

"In The Long Ago, Earth Mother shook hard in these islands. Sea sucked away from the shore, rushed out to seaskyline, and returned as a huge wave, bringing creatures too helpless to escape—even great whales—all the way up Spirit Mountain. Great Whale got tossed ashore where he tangled in tree branches. He couldn't swim free. He couldn't breathe. Great Spirit looked down and saw the huge, sleek whale, a dear friend, thrashing and felt pity. Great Spirit called upon Earth Mother to calm the sea and shouted: 'Save yourself, Whale. Of all my creatures, I chose you to be of dual nature: wolf on land, whale in sea. It's your birthright. Use it now. Quickly!'

   D Y A N   D U B O I S

"The great black-and-white whale jumped and flipped, slashed and shook. Hair grew where sleek skin had been. Paddle-shaped flippers became straight forelegs. Tail fins became furry hind legs. Small teeth grew to large fangs. Whale's black eyes turned gold. A bushy tail sprouted. A snout jutted out where the blowhole had been. Whale became a wolf. He rose on all fours and shook water from his thick fur. Great Spirit commanded: 'From this time forth, hear my decree—wolf on land, whale in sea—but when you change is up to me.'"

The mention of a great wave scared WolfShe. She twitched. She looked at Ama, but Ama's attention turned to Chief Lightning Bolt. He walked to the firepit and said to the crowd, "Earth-shakes and great floods, omens from Great Spirit, warn us to be alert. Change is coming."

The elders hummed in agreement. Children squirmed. Ama nodded. WolfShe saw Ama's brow go up like a mountain peak, and her head tilt toward WolfShe as a warning to the chief to halt his words.

WolfShe blurted out: "What omens?"

The gathering stared at her. WolfShe looked around the fire circle, wondering if their hard gazes condemned her for asking, or feared what she might say. She wished she could suck the words back into her throat and swallow them. But they hung in the air, rising with the flames, filling the night with orange sparks of apprehension.

"You don't know, young Medicine Woman? Ama never mentioned the omens?" The chief glanced over at Ama with a quizzical expression. "You should know. Tonight, you learn. Tomorrow, you will see more clearly. I can tell you in my boyhood days, we received an omen. It was in early spring. Chill winds blew. A great canoe appeared at sea-skyline. Our people were working, repairing nets on the beach. Never had we seen such a sight, a large canoe with great white fins. People watched the fins flutter like fish gills when the breeze faltered and bloat like a pregnant elk when the wind shifted. We wondered, what did Great Spirit bring us?

"Many gathered to watch. We built fires. Flames rose high in the raging wind. Some prepared a feast, thinking Great Spirit brought a gift. Others ran for bow and arrows, harpoons, and seal clubs. Questions chewed the air: Which tribe? Which island? What do they bring? What do they want? The sea curled high and tossed the large canoe side to side. White fins fluttered and fell like fledging birds into the water. Many braves refused to row out to the white-fin canoe in such dangerous waves. Others insisted we must find out who rides this storm to our shore. Twelve men paddled out in our largest whaling canoe. They crested the waves, dropped from sight, crested again. The sea grew angrier. Huge waves slammed the beach.

"The canoe rounded the spit at River Mouth near the rocks. Our canoe swung wide in the choppy water, avoiding the cliffs. White-fin canoe hit one rock, then another. Planks cried like seagulls. Wood split. Water rushed into the canoe's belly. White-fin rocked side to side, slapped the water, and collapsed on its side. Men slipped and jumped into the cold, gray water, screaming. Waves tossed them against the rocks. They screeched like hawks. Heads popped up in the angry sea and sunk from sight. Our canoe rowed toward the drowning men. Braves cast their fishing nets, caught the men, and dragged them on shore.

"Women grabbed their children and dragged them home. Braves made fires on the beach to warm the strange men spit out by the sea. The intruders shouted sharp noises and poked at their mouths, pretending to chew. At our chief's command, braves roasted salmon on fire rocks and fed them. They said no blessing to Salmon People before stuffing the pink flesh into their mouths. The men were pale like fish bellies. Maybe this is how they die, we thought. A White-Belly handed my father a heavy, dark ring attached to a shard of wood. Father told me he almost dropped it. Braves inspected the object's rough, hard, cold skin. No one knew what it was.

"Those men were Two-Leggeds…but different. Pale skin, eyes like seawater, and with matted hair the color of cedar bark, or clumped brown earth, or sun-yellowed weeds. They made growls and grunts we couldn't understand. Their face and lips, cracked from sun and saltwater, bled red like ours. They smelled rotten. We gave them clothes to wear.

"At sunrise, our braves built huge fires and fed White-Bellies. We kept them away from the village. They had no knives, spears, harpoons, or clubs. They were harmless and weak—dying, we thought. We walked them to where white-fin jutted from the rocks. They found pieces like the strong, hard circle. They threw it into the fire. It glowed red-hot but didn't burn. They threw the piece in water. It hissed and turned black. We beat it with rocks. It didn't break. They called it *metul*. My father wanted *metul*. We traded many items—baskets, bowls, colored beads, fishing nets, food, and cedar-cloth—for their *metul*.

"Tribal council met on the full moon to discuss the White-Belly tribe. We decided we must drive them away. Our women feared them. White-Bellies watched our women like hawks watch field mice. They had grown strong on our food. They shouted and shoved a young brave to the sand. When his father jumped in to help him, a White-Belly cut him. The White-Bellies attacked us. Our braves tied them together and walked them many sunrises, up, down, and around on mountain paths, across streams, through forests, and backtracked in circles to confuse them. We left them at low tide, in the far north-east point, where a narrow land bridge connects to the mainland for two sunrises every harvest season. Some of our braves wanted to kill them. Most wanted to leave that to mainland tribes. 'Why waste our effort?' chief said. 'They don't know how to survive. They will not last long.' Before releasing them, our braves shouted at the White-Belly men, scraped their knives across their throats, slitting the skin enough to draw blood, and warned them never to return, or they would die. White-Bellies shook. They understood. They ran. We watched the narrow path until the sea rushed in again to bury it. In ceremony, we discovered they were an omen. 'Of what?' we asked. 'Of what would come,' shaman replied.

"Many harvest seasons passed before the earth rumbled and that northwest point slipped into the sea. The path-way to the mainland disappeared. We held ceremony and believed the omen had been fulfilled. We could feel safe. I grew to manhood and had three sons by the time the Great Flood came. I wondered: Was the omen related to the Great Flood? I had thought so, but now I wonder."

Chief Lightning Bolt looked at WolfShe. "You know of what I speak. White-Belly caused Earth Mother to cry. She stopped those men from reaching our shore by crash-ing their canoe onto rocks, but we saved them. We didn't understand the omen she had shown us: White-Belly brings trouble."

     Dyan Dubois

WolfShe hung her head and nodded *yes*.

"Many wonder about you, WolfShe. Why did Earth Mother spit you out? Running Bear's grandfather says you saved him, gave more days to his earth-walk. But danger comes with you. The Pale Face trapper threatens Wolf People…and he looks for you. Are you an omen? We must rid our land of Pale Face, so Earth Mother does not cry again."

WolfShe's head jerked up. "Pale Face looks for me?"

"Pale Face tracks you and your wolf. He knows you saved Three-Legged. Some say your wolf is a demon, others say a healing spirit. But you and Ama left your cabin in the woods to move into our village. We are glad to have you closer. Did someone scare you? Is that why you came? What do you know?"

An old woman shuffled forward and circled WolfShe, fanning the air with smoldering cedar bough. WolfShe pulled the blessed smoke to her face. The elder chanted the prayer of protection. WolfShe stared at Ama, who clutched her hands so tightly that white knuckles erupted from her brown skin. But Ama didn't look up.

"I know he kills wolves for their pelts."

WolfShe had not feared the pale-faced trapper…until now. He has the power of an evil omen. He wears a cloak of fog and wolf pelts, so he can hide in the woods. WolfShe knew demons walk upright as easily as they slither. She wondered, Could he be Black Snake in disguise? Does he come from the Land of Shadow Fog, a place too cruel to imagine, and too frightening. She winced. She looked to Ama for reassurance, but Ama's eyes rested on her brittle hands.

WolfShe sat, silently remembering the pain *metul* teeth had inflicted on her gray wolf, swearing that Pale Face will never succeed. She thought, He must leave our land. I will drive him out. He will not kill again. This I pledge to Great Spirit.

"Honorable Chief, we moved here because I wanted Ama to enjoy her friends, to have an easier life. Living out in the woods became too hard. I serve better being near the people I care for. I know Pale Face roams our forest and brings evil to our land. We must guard against him."

"And your wolf?"

"He is my protector, and I am his."

Ama looked up. WolfShe saw a smile part her lips.

"Chief Lightning Bolt," Ama began, "Pale Face trapped the wolf. WolfShe saved him. The animal watches over WolfShe and our tribe. If anyone sees Three-Legged, leave him alone. Great Spirit sent him to help, not hurt. Pale Face is the evil omen. Great Spirit and Earth Mother blessed us with a good omen, the three-legged wolf."

The chief nodded. "We see these signs. We will learn their meaning. The return of a White-Belly using *metul* is a warning. Something comes. We must discover what."

❦

WolfShe studied wolf tracks in mountain and forest, looked for dens, observed hunting behaviors, and learned to identify paw impressions and scat for individual wolves, Three-Legged's being the easiest. Traveling with Three-Legged allowed her to predict Pale Face's killing strategy and thwart it.

In late spring, when she and her wolf came upon a den, she dropped back to watch, but Three-Legged trotted ahead. He yipped. A chorus of small barks answered. A she-wolf rushed out to meet him, dropped to her belly and rolled over in submission, before edging close to lick his mouth. WolfShe saw her milk-swollen teats. Three-Legged bared his fangs when five pups, tripping over each other, scrambled out of a hole in the ground to greet him. He nibbled their necks and nudged them.

WolfShe sat quietly watching the family scene. She recalled the day her world changed, the day she and Three-Legged began communicating. It wasn't like this with nips and nudges. She had touched his thick fur mantle. He didn't shy away. The charcoal-gray fur slid between her fingers. He looked up at her with steady golden eyes. He nudged her with his muzzle. That day, when wolf looked at her eyes, WolfShe heard something impressed on her—not in animal sounds—but in thoughts. She touched his jowls and felt the soft exhale of his warm breath. Wolf made no other sound, yet WolfShe understood: *Pale Face hunts us*. She remembered how quickly she had dropped her hands from his neck ruffle, like a live coal, jumped up and spun around but saw no one.

Watching Three-Legged's pups roll and tumble, nipping each other, unaware of her presence, she heard impressed in her thoughts: *Run! Trapper!* Her head jerked up. Three-Legged bolted, herding his family into the den. He grabbed a lagging pup by the scruff and dragged him into the den. They disappeared, hidden by undergrowth, moss-covered fallen trees, and shadows. WolfShe froze. She listened. She smelled the trapper's acrid stench. Her nose wrinkled. She crouched low in the bracken next to a massive, fallen cedar tree to watch and wait.

Pale Face poked his staff into the earth as he walked. She heard the thump, thump, thump before she spotted him. He stopped. He reached down and lifted a handful of forest litter to his nose. He surveyed the bracken. He began walking in WolfShe's direction. She squatted, ready to bolt, waiting to see if he veered away. He turned abruptly toward the den. He slammed his staff down in the foliage, crushing bracken out of his way, picked up a handful of dirt, and sniffed again. Eyes cast to the ground, he wheeled around to face her direction.

She darted from her hiding place and ran along her honey-gathering path. She ran fast like an elk, cut back into dense forest, and looped east…away from the den. She squatted, waiting. When twigs snapped, she stood. Pale Face spotted her. He waved his hand.

To her surprise, he shouted in native tongue. "Medicine Woman. I see you." WolfShe grunted like a wild pig but remained still, gauging the distance between them. "Friend. Talk," he shouted, drawing closer.

WolfShe looked into his frozen-stream eyes. She trembled thinking: demon eyes. She leaped up and sailed over the soft ground, her feet hardly touching the earth. The tracker shouted and chased her, struggling to follow her up-mountain—away from Three-Legged's den—to the craggy-rocks home of Cougar People. Rid our land of this pale-faced demon, WolfShe prayed, for all of us.

CHAPTER SEVEN

Running Bear

Since the encounter with Pale Face, WolfShe knew nothing of him. She believed Cougar People had done their job. She put him out of her thoughts and reveled in the warmth and light of growing season. The sun felt like warm honey on her arms—soft, comforting, sweet—but not sticky and not hard to reach. But soon heat sickness would arrive for babies, elders, and the weak. Mild days gave way to wavy heat piled high with thunder clouds. No wind stirred the night.

WolfShe was grateful Ama could still tolerate the heat at her age, but she reminded her to drink water often. Ama smiled and said, "This weather makes me feel good…no pain when I stand and move. No loud popping! Don't worry about me."

On a walk to their neighbor's, WolfShe said, "No sea breeze for seven sunrises. The earth's a firepit. I can't remember so much heat, Ama. Do you think the braves will burn the meadow grass near your cabin this season? It's grown tall since we moved."

"Don't know. They have so much work. We'll have to collect beach grass earlier than usual. Too much sun weakens the fibers, not good for weaving, too weedy, can't tie knots. Everything will wither if this heat continues. They won't have time for my meadow. I don't have the strength, and you don't have the time either with your medicine duties. Then there's the summer catch. This summer is rushing to harvest too early."

WolfShe noticed Ama stood straighter now, had spring in her gait. WolfShe thought, Ama will go on forever. At that moment, a dark cloud passed overhead, sweeping her heart with raven wing shadows.

"WolfShe? Shivering in this heat?"

"Ama, there's…something I never told you."

"Speak."

"I don't want to upset you, Ama."

"Am I too old to hear your heart?"

"No. But you have more important things to think about."

"Nothing more important than you. Is it Running Bear? I know he likes you very much, but you ignore him. He needs encouragement, or he may look elsewhere for a wife. He's a good choice for you, WolfShe, kind and loving."

"Ama! A choice for me? That sounds like you want me to marry and move into his longhouse. That's not what I wanted to talk about."

"I do want you to marry before I depart for the Land of Mists. I want to see you settled and cared for, so I can join my ancestors in peace, my duty done, my life complete."

WolfShe wrapped her arm around Ama and whispered, "We are complete."

The old woman steadied herself firmly in front of WolfShe. "Your heart has grown, Daughter. Let others in. Get to know Running Bear. You will like him, even love him…someday. He's a good provider. They are a good family. You came from the woods alone, but now you should live in a longhouse where many will love and protect you. That is my only wish. I dream of what you will do in your long life. Let people know you. Visit, talk, laugh, dance, be part of his family and our village. I will go in peace, blessed by Great Spirit, if you will do that for me, WolfShe."

"I care for the sick. I bring new babes to their mother's arms. I visit elders, hear their troubles, treat their illnesses. That shows the villagers who I am. I don't need to dance and chatter. Ama, I am who I am."

"Who is that? A woman with a wolf companion who slips into the forest and shuns men? People fear you, WolfShe. They say you only love that wolf…and me. They say the wolf has possessed you and will turn you into something not human. They say your wolf lured Pale Face here, to our land, and someday will eat him for dinner…and then eat the entire village."

WolfShe wanted to laugh, but the concern etched in Ama's brow scared her. She bit her lip. "Ama, what I've kept from you since we moved into the village is that Pale Face tracked the wolf and me. He may have died. I don't know. I led him up to the craggy rocks. Maybe Cougar People took care of him? I patrol, but I haven't seen him. I must live as I do to protect the village. A mate would only get in my way."

Ama gasped. "He tracked you?"

"He spoke to me in native tongue. Ama, let's sit under the trees by the stream. The heat has scorched you."

They settled down in the shade. Ama lowered herself slowly to her haunches.

WolfShe thought to tell Ama all she knew of the intruder, but she held back. She wanted to brag, The trapper doesn't see me because I'm quicker, quieter. He spotted me once, but I outran him. Instead, she reassured Ama, saying Great Spirit blesses her with speed. She outruns elk. Wind lifts her up. She doesn't leave tracks. When she looked at the rain in Ama's clouded eyes, she said no more. She didn't recount what the fisherman told her when she stitched his ripped hand, the story of a trapper he'd seen at the far north point, a man with no color, even in his eyes, whose canoe was filled with animal furs—weasel, beaver, cougar. Local traders whispered they'd seen others like him.

Ama rubbed her tired eyes and looked at WolfShe. "You are not like us. You never were. Great Spirit gave you abilities others don't have. But you lack understanding, especially about danger. Cedar-hair pale-face demon tracks you, not to stop you from springing his *metul* traps, but to harm you. WolfShe, he could force his man-ness on you, attack you in ways you don't understand. He can't catch you, or stop you, or prevent you from freeing his traps…yet. But he won't give up. He grows more and more dangerous, vicious like a wounded cougar, every time you trick him. When he does pounce, he will pounce hard."

"How do you know this, Ama?"

"The ancestors have spoken. They said he won't catch you if you choose a husband and live in his family long-house as the wise woman healer you are meant to be. Let the braves deal with Pale Face. Think of me, Daughter. How can I travel to the Land of Mists worrying about you?" Ama's shoulders dropped. She leaned forward, grasped her knees to her chest, and sobbed.

WolfShe winced, hearing Ama's choppy breaths. She feared Ama might not catch her next one. "Ama, yes, I agree to Running Bear, but I won't be his wife, yet. I will decide the time. I will work long days as medicine woman, join potlatches, speak to people, as you wish. But I must track Pale Face in our forest. That's all, follow his tracks, so I can inform Running Bear and the braves where to hunt him."

Ama rubbed her face dry with her tunic. "Don't wait, WolfShe." Ama brushed tendrils of wavy hair away from WolfShe's face. "Many depend on you. What good are you snared? What good are you if Pale Face ruins you?"

WolfShe felt a heavy stone press her into dark water. The concern in Ama's pleading eyes made her shiver in the heat. She wondered, Can Ama see my death? The look triggered a vision that had haunted her since her wild years, being helpless when a predator approached. Now the vision stared at her through Ama's eyes. WolfShe's chest fell. She sighed. "Ama, I will ask Running Bear to go with me when I gather. I won't go alone. That way we can become friends. I will teach him plant harvesting and honey gathering. I will learn something useful from him. I will teach him…"

"*Metul* trap?"

"Yes, he must learn to avoid traps, like every forest walker. I will put skunk cabbage potion in our forest to ward Wolf People away. Pale Face travels low in the forest. Wolf People will stay high, above the tree line. He will tire of empty traps and go away." As WolfShe spoke the words, she felt their falseness. She knew Pale Face would not give up.

"Don't think cedar-hair is stupid. He understands wolf habits. He knows where to bury killing teeth and how to follow prints—of animals and people—by the shape of the pads, the depth of foot impressions, and their size. He recognizes yours. Even if you say your feet don't touch the ground when you run, they do when you stand to release his traps. Try your potion, but the first rain will wash it away. Maybe it will help a little. Sometimes Great Spirit's wish is a test: which creature is ready for spirit and which is meant to stay with Earth Mother. And that includes you, WolfShe."

"Yes, Ama," WolfShe replied. She realized surviving the Great Flood had meaning, and she believed she had found hers: defeat the Pale Face trapper.

⁓

WolfShe worked hard. Warm, sunny days had rallied life from winter-dormant soil. Bright-green sprouts grew quickly and swelled in the heat. WolfShe stayed away from the forest shadows. She spent her time in the open meadow gathering herbs for decoctions, digging up edible bulbs, picking early berries, and cutting sedges for Ama's basket weaving. Her mood shifted. She hadn't realized how the blackness in her mind had ruled her. She loved digging earth; inhaling the moist scent of decayed wood, dried leaves, and sweet grasses; and dozing in the sun.

She invited village women to work alongside her. She taught them simple methods of gathering medicine herbs, preserving their healing properties, and starting their own home medicine baskets. No one spoke of the trapper—or her wolf—but they whispered among themselves. Pale Face gave up and returned to his demon land because WolfShe drove him away. WolfShe smiled, hearing the whispers, and prayed, knowing their words didn't match what the fisherman had reported. She prayed the women were right.

Ama sat in the women's circle to weave fishnets for the salmon catch while the men spent long days tending fish traps in the river and rowing canoes out to sea, hunting whales and sea lions. Running Bear worked along the river, not far from River Bend Village, but had no time to visit WolfShe. WolfShe looked forward to First Catch Ceremony and dinner when everyone would bless Salmon People, burying their first-catch bones to offer thanks. She hoped to speak to Running Bear. She wanted to feel the warmth he radiated, to smell his scent.

When the celebration arrived, WolfShe wove colored beads into her long braids and put on the new tunic Ama had made her with small rounds of abalone shell decorating the neck. Ama had said for good luck. WolfShe knew she meant with Running Bear. When she spotted Running Bear serving the elders roasted salmon from the fire, she smiled. Running Bear beamed. After the last elder was served, he rushed to WolfShe. He placed a carved wooden bowl filled with salmon and roasted lily bulbs in WolfShe's hands.

"So much?" WolfShe said, looking up at him, realizing for the first time how tall Running Bear had grown.

Running Bear smiled. "We share."

Ama scooted over and motioned for him to sit beside WolfShe while she continued telling her friend a fishing story from her youth. When she rose on creaking knees, Running Bear jumped up to offer his hand. Ama smiled at him. With one eyebrow cocked upward, and a sideways tip of her head, she glanced at WolfShe and ambled away to the elder women circle.

Running Bear sat close to WolfShe, so close their skin touched. She felt the warmth of him. She didn't move. She shook her head to rouse from the sleepy feeling of having his body next to hers. They ate in silence from the shared bowl. Their silence roared like spring-thaw plummeting over rocks. She wondered: Does Running Bear hear this?

"Today you gathered medicine plants?"

WolfShe pulled back from the humming sound that overwhelmed her, and replied, "Some now, more later."

"In the forest?"

"Why do you ask? No, the meadow."

"I want to learn medicine plants. I thought you could teach me."

"Yes, I would like that. Some grow in rotting logs; some—fern roots and moss—like shade. Others thrive in meadow soil and sun."

"Can I go with you soon? Grandfather said it would be good for me to learn."

WolfShe smiled, thinking how similar his grandfather and Ama were. "Yes, you can help me. I would like that. I will also teach you wound care, stitching, and cleaning."

"I was on a canoe-hunting trip when a harpoon tip cut a brave's leg. He bled so much we thought he wouldn't make it to shore."

"Did he?"

"Yes. We wrapped the leg in tight rope, and a brave sat on the wound to slow the blood. Then Ama treated him. He recovered to fish and walk."

"I stay away from the sea. I won't go into seawater."

"Rivers?"

"Rivers I like…and streams."

"WolfShe, let me row you upriver from Green Valley to a broad stretch of calm, sweet water that follows the forest opposite your favorite meadow. I think you don't cross that river often. You should see it. Trees have water twins. You can't tell them apart on a calm day."

"I would like to see that and learn to row a canoe."

"The river's safer than the forest you roam, WolfShe. Be careful. Don't go alone. There's word that Pale Face was seen."

WolfShe jumped and broke the warmth of their touch. "Pale Face left," she said.

"When you hid his *metul* teeth traps, he left…but only to get more traps."

"Who says that? How would they know?"

"Three-Legged, your wolf."

"He doesn't talk."

"He did, to Chief Lightning Bolt, when the moon's face turned black and the hair around it shone silver in the night sky. The council held a special sweat lodge. Your wolf's spirit appeared."

"Why didn't someone tell me?"

"The council chose not to, but they told Ama. We thought she had told you."

"She didn't. Did he say anything…about me?"

"He warned more like Pale Face would come. They have no belief in Great Spirit, no belief in animal spirits, no belief in earth spirits, not even Earth Mother. They worship a creator no one sees. They don't know Raven People, Salmon People, Elk People, swimmers, fliers—only Two-Leggeds like themselves, pale and foul smelling. Shaman says they understand nothing. They are like blind rats in the sun. They come to take what they want. They give nothing. We must protect ourselves."

"How do we prepare?"

"Shaman doesn't know. He said they bring change. An ill north wind blows. He smells it coming over the sea. He said Wolf People wait and watch in the forest. In the meadows Elk People stand guard. In the mountains Cougar People and Bear People search the hills. Whale People watch the waters. No one wants them."

WolfShe jumped like a wasp had stung her. "Running Bear, when can you go with me into the forest?"

Running Bear stood. "The braves and I are greasing the

new whaling canoe for our first run. I will come to you in three sunrises. Do not go without me."

Running Bear leaned toward WolfShe, so close she thought she felt his heartbeat touch her tunic. He smiled, looked into her eyes, and walked away. She watched his muscular stride but looked down quickly when he joined the braves' circle by the fire. Running Bear's father turned to look at her. She hung her head. Out of the corner of her eye, she saw him smile.

WolfShe felt like the last rays of sun flowed over her like amber honey. She caught Running Bear's scent—cedar, sweet meadow grass, and damp earth. Her face burned. She rushed to join the women and children laughing and talking around the fire. When Running Bear looked her way, she wondered why she couldn't hear him like she could her wolf. He brushed the hawk-feather braid back from his face. He smiled at her. The hairs on her forearm rose. She scrunched her toes in her soft boots. She couldn't *hear* him, but she could feel him.

The storyteller called people over. WolfShe motioned for Ama to sit beside her. The old storyteller shook his rattles, stamped his feet, and let out a long, low whistle to gather the attention of jabbering children and adults.

"Little people, listen well, and learn. Great Spirit sent the first people Star Child. Star Child taught us what to eat, which plants to use for medicine, which for food, and which poison the body. Star Child taught us fishing, canoe-making, bow-and-arrow skills...so many things. Star Child taught us to make tools, weave cedar ropes, make watertight baskets, carve dolls and toys for you children. He gave your mothers knowledge to care for you, guide you, make you honest. But you, children, you do

 DYAN DUBOIS

not always listen, just like a boy named Loon Boy didn't listen. Hear his story."

WolfShe's head popped up. She recalled her mother telling her the story of Loon Boy. WolfShe saw herself as a very young child. She felt cool sand squish between her toes where gentle waves curled and tickled the sand away. Her mother pointed to a long tube of sea kelp bobbing on the water's surface like the head of a sea lion popping up and diving down with the waves.

She heard her mother say, "Look, she's been here, the girl who married the man of the sea. Sea kelp marks where she came ashore. When the beautiful young girl met him, they fell in love. She followed him to his home deep in the sea. But she still returns to see her loving mother, father, sisters, and brothers. She leaves a kelp trail." Her mother's dark eyes glowed with setting sun. WolfShe could smell wet camas, sweet and calm, clinging to her mother's tunic. She heard her child voice whisper, "I won't ever leave you, *Maaha*. I won't go to the bottom of the sea."

A loud rap of the storyteller's wooden stick on drum leather, the shaking of olivella shells, and a loud whoop wrenched WolfShe's attention back to the fire circle.

"If you don't listen, children, you could be in trouble," the storyteller said, tucking his chin. "Loon Boy's mother said, 'Son, never go to Mason Lake. It's haunted.'" The storyteller stamped his feet and waved an eagle feather whisk in the air. "Well, the boy didn't listen to his mother. He was naughty and headstrong. She warned him, never swim in Mason Lake. Did you hear her warn him?" The children nodded *yes*. "Did he listen?" The children nodded *no*. The storyteller stomped his feet, making his shell anklets jingle.

"The boy went anyway. He wanted to catch a trout. But

the trout was really an evil spirit. The evil trout-demon changed the boy into a loon. The poor boy called and called to his mother to help him, to save him, in his bird voice, but all she heard was a loon squawking. Poor boy. Poor mother. They couldn't understand each other's cries.

"So, children, listen to your mothers, so you don't end up like Loon Boy." The elder swished eagle feathers over the fire circle, stomping his feet, and shouted, "Honor your mother. Listen to her. Great Spirit gave you a mother to guide you, so you can become strong and honest."

Little children clung to their mother's tunics, afraid to move. The storyteller beat his drum. The circle broke. Mothers and children drifted away. WolfShe sat stunned, wondering if there was a message in the story for her. No, a story is a story, she told herself…or a warning?

⁓⁓⁓

DAYS PASSED. SHE WALKED THE SHORE, STARING AT THE sea. Bobbing kelp heads on the waves appeared and disappeared. The same thought from the fire circle kept haunting her. Are you waiting for me, Maaha? How do I find you? Give me a sign I can follow. WolfShe sighed and picked up olivella shells. She stopped abruptly, spotting a purple-gray one in the sand. She often found tan olivellas, but a shell double in size, the color of early dawn was rare, too rare to be an accident. It was a sign. WolfShe heard a whisper on the wind: *what you seek seeks you.*

Later that morning, walking the footpath toward the meadow below Sacred Mountain, WolfShe spotted Running Bear approaching at a swift pace, his braid slapping side to side. She asked him, "When you hunt sea lions, do you see anyone in the water?"

He looked at her, took a breath, and said, "No. Only fish, never Two-Leggeds. Whale People swim under our canoes at times."

WolfShe realized how stupid her question sounded. "Yes, that's what I meant, Whale People. Lucky you, I've never seen a whale up close. So, what work do you do today? I didn't think I would see you."

"I'm checking basket traps along the river before sundown. Father told me to help with your work and walk you home. You shouldn't be here alone."

WolfShe felt deflated. She thought Running Bear had chosen to visit her. "I like to harvest on my own. You'd said you would take me upriver when you set nets. Remember?"

"We'll do that but not today."

WolfShe stepped back, straightened the basket on her back, and increased her pace, cutting him off. "I don't need help. If that's what your father thinks, he's wrong."

"Slow down, WolfShe. I have a message. *Be watchful.*"

WolfShe stopped abruptly and wheeled around to face Running Bear. "Of what?"

"*Hokwat.* Father says he heard reports of drifting-house people. No one has seen Pale Face, but a runner from the north reported *hokwats* had crossed the strait. The council worries for you."

"Me? We should worry for us all and every Four-Legged of the forest…also Three."

"The runner said two crushed *hokwat* canoes washed ashore at the northwest point. The braves of Whale Water Village tracked the men. Four Pale Faces walked along the shore, eating gull eggs, crab, and fish. The people of Whale Water held ceremony and called on spirits to take them deep into the sea and devour them. Two died. The other two left their bodies to rot on the beach. Scavengers picked their ugly flesh. What kind of humans have no blessing ceremony for the dead?"

"Left their bodies on our beach? Their evil spirits roam our land," WolfShe said and shook involuntarily. "They will steal a living body, so they can live among us, killing and feeding on our spirits."

"WolfShe, there's more. Cedar-hair Pale Face…he's one of them. The elders fear for you."

A cold shiver clenched her spine. She whispered, "Why?"

"You travel with the wolf he hates. He wants you. You cannot roam—or be alone—that is their demand."

WolfShe felt a wave of bitterness sear her throat. She doubled over, her basket knocking into the back of her head. She gasped like the air had been knocked out of her. Running Bear yanked the basket off and placed his palm between her shoulder blades. WolfShe felt a rush of buzzing heat run up her back. She arched and faced Running Bear, eyes wide, lips open to speak, but no words came.

Running Bear shook. "I just saw something…horrible, WolfShe. Your hands were covered with blood."

WolfShe shook her hands like she was throwing something off. "Running Bear, you had a vision. Where was I?"

"In the forest, near three huge rocks. You screamed. You stared at your hands, screaming. Water ran from your eyes. You were afraid."

WolfShe slumped to the ground. Running Bear wrapped his arms around her and pulled her tight to his chest. He swayed her back and forth. When she looked up at him, WolfShe felt a cord in her vibrate like a bow string after the arrow releases. She steadied herself, found her footing, hoisted the basket onto her back, adjusted the leather band at her forehead, and walked away without uttering a word. Running Bear followed.

"Drink," he commanded when she finally slowed her pace, shoving the water bladder into her hand. He pulled a packet from his satchel and tore smoked salmon into pieces. "Eat."

WolfShe raked her tongue across sun-chapped lips and gulped water. "I can do this, Running Bear. I will finish Pale Face."

"No! Pale-faced invaders aren't like us. You are a medicine woman, our healer. Leave him to us braves." Running Bear grabbed her by the wrist. "Look at me. We will protect you."

"He's the Black Snake. He brings evil."

"I will watch over you," Running Bear said and offered a timid smile. "If you let me, we will never part." His dark eyebrows inched up to the hawk feather woven into his braid. "Today Pale Face is in the northwest. What work do you have?"

"The yew grove."

"We will work together. Mother wants new spoons, the braves—bows and harpoon shafts."

They walked in silence to the grove. WolfShe wondered how they could haul that much wood. She needed only pulp for wound care, a task she could handle alone. Her thoughts spooked like sparrows, but Running Bear's presence calmed her.

"What can I carve for you? Hair comb? Arrows? Trinket box?"

"I have those," WolfShe said and watched a dark cloud pass over Running Bear's smile. Realizing she had hurt him, she said, "Yes, a new comb. Mine has broken teeth. I would like one very much, one made by you."

They stopped at the berry patch, so WolfShe could pick late season salmonberries, and then continued to the yew tree grove. She watched Running Bear hack yew branches into a large pile. Her thoughts drifted to Ama's ancestors. Had they harvested the same patch of berries, hacked the same trees? she wondered. When Ama joins her ancestors in the Land of Mists, they will greet her at the gate with blessings. Who will meet me? Sadness descended on her, a chilling fog. She worried she would stand at the entrance to the Land of Mists but never find the opening, never walk through the gate, never receive the blessings her people and totem could bestow. She feared dark spirits would grab her, drag her down into the Land of Shadow Fog, the place of darkness and regret, the home of Black Snake. WolfShe chewed these thoughts, tasted their bitterness, and grew despondent.

Running Bear walked toward her with late afternoon sun glistening on his damp forehead. "How will we carry the wood?"

"I can carry great weight," she snapped.

"No one doubts that, especially me." Running Bear scratched a pattern in the dirt with his stick and didn't look up. "You go from healer to something else. Who are you, WolfShe? You treat the sick with kindness, nurse them back to health. I see you, at other times, fierce as a wild animal, like now, but I have done nothing."

WolfShe burst out, "I am a wild half-human/half-animal. I have no ancestors to count on. I last glimpsed my mother in a canoe, water pouring over us, heard her screaming, saw my baby sister slip from *Maaha*'s grip and get swallowed by the sea. I don't remember what my mother named me. My name washed away that day, like so many other things, gone with the sea. I am not Ama's clan. I'm not your clan, Running Bear. I see your people, good people, but I don't understand them…or you. I have no totem. I had no naming ceremony and never will. Ama called me wolf girl because I was wild like a wolf in the woods. I stand alone."

Running Bear looked away. In the distance, jagged peaks pierced flat-bottom clouds. He turned back to look directly into WolfShe's eyes. "You could join my clan, my family. Many respect you; my family respects you. Ama trained you. She made you hers. I will make you mine."

WolfShe squeezed her eyebrows into a dark line that bridged her fierce eyes. She clamped her teeth so hard a sharp pain stabbed her ear. She spat out, "I am mine! Your people accept my medicine work…not *me*. Be careful of what you say. Words are binding, Running Bear, like ropes."

"WolfShe, I choose you."

WolfShe gasped and stumbled backward, the weight of her basket throwing her off. She righted herself. "Your life mate? Why?"

"Men and women work together, help and protect each other, have children. I want you."

The words rushed like snowmelt in her veins coursing back to her heart. "I'm cursed, Running Bear. Children would carry my shame."

"I see what you are," Running Bear said with a smile, a shallow indentation dividing his chin. "Beauty. Power. A fiery sunset that touches green waves and makes them glow. A soft feather blanket on a cold night. A fierce defender. A healer."

"Pretty words, Running Bear. You should be prayer-elder someday."

WolfShe saw something move in the distance, a shadow

weaving through the trees. Wolf? In daylight? Running Bear followed her line of sight and withdrew his knife.

"No. Running Bear, my wolf, he watches."

"I know…but who does he watch? He knows I would never hurt you. You saved an elder in River Mouth Village last spring. He told the council you would be shaman someday because he saw a wolf spirit standing over you when you treated him. The wolf begged Great Spirit for more time for the old man. He needed to complete an obligation to his wife. Great Spirit granted that wish. The elder told the council your wolf spirit stood upright on hind legs like the legendary Justice Wolves. Ama requested the elder not speak of that again, fearing people might think you a halfling-spirit, not fully human, part wolf. WolfShe, I see that gray wolf hiding in the shadows up there. Great Spirit gave him to you as a gift. The proof stands strong in you. Healer, not destroyer; wise woman, not trickster. Don't let fears torment you. Our children will have ancestors. They will carry our Bear family totem. I choose you to be my life mate."

"I'm too young."

"We're both young. We could have our promise potlatch at the end of harvest season, and our union at next harvest potlatch."

WolfShe studied Running Bear. He had everything she could imagine in a mate—strength, kindness, family, and a pleasing aroma of cedar, sunlight, and meadow grass—but her life would change with him…because of him. She didn't want anyone watching her secret ways, stealing into the forest to be with her wolf, springing *metul* traps, tracking Pale Face. A vision of growing old quietly sitting by a fire, watching sparks rise, glimmer, and disappear made her sad.

"When blossoms return to the meadow again, we will again speak of this."

Running Bear smiled and patted her shoulder. WolfShe's face warmed to his touch. She questioned how he brought the sun so quickly, even in cool air. She wondered, Would Running Bear's warmth always flow to her, or would it turn to an icy winter stream?

"Grandfather's special gift, the bow and arrows, do you use it? He made it from a sacred yew tree, one that stood for many years before the Great Flood."

"Running Bear, you should use it. I can't kill anything, not for food, not for skins."

"For protection?"

"I think the more you learn of me, the less you will choose union."

"Let me decide. Until then, I'll teach you bow and arrow. Don't worry, you will never shoot as well as me, but you may be good someday."

"I'll be better than my teacher," WolfShe said with a grin. "But I will never shoot an animal."

Running Bear cocked his head to the side. "Look uphill. Your wolf waits. Want to go to him?"

"He'll run if you approach."

"He's clever. I saw Three-Legged when you treated Grandfather. No one else did. That was the second time I saw him. Earlier, in winter short days, I had walked the mountain, hunting rabbit. I found his tracks. I followed them to the bubbling hot water rocks under Jagged Peak. He stood above me on a cliff, watching. A powerful wolf, even on three legs, with a dark coat like obsidian, shiny and thick. His gold eyes watched me. He tracked me down the mountain and turned to leave when I reached the meadow.

I decided that day, I will name our first son Running Wolf."

"What? You planned our children seasons ago? Wolf wanted you to know something. Otherwise, you would have never seen him."

"A day may come, WolfShe, when that wolf may talk to you if he is your totem—not your curse."

CHAPTER EIGHT

Raven-Shadow

Winter had been hard on Ama—too cold, too long, too damp. WolfShe watched Ama's life-stream diminish to a meandering creek, her breathing lessen to a whisper, her eye whites turn pink like yew tree bark. She did everything she could to make Ama comfortable.

A thought nagged at WolfShe. Did worrying about her weaken Ama? The night she spoke of seeing Black Snake again, curled in the darkness of the obsidian lake, Ama shook and told her not to use that name in her house. She said to speak of evil was to invite evil.

WolfShe roused Ama from a nap. "Ama, I made a rich broth of blue camas, tiger lily, and onion bulbs for you. Smoked salmon's in the basket. I won't be away long. A message came from Camas Creek, a child has high fever. Stay near the fire and keep warm. I will return before dark."

"Don't forget your knife and medicine bag, WolfShe."

"No, Ama. I won't. After all these years, you still remind me. I thought since I would be on the creek, I should harvest tender camas."

"Running Bear, does he go with you?"

"Not today, Ama. He's repairing nets with his father."

"WolfShe, he hasn't come here for days. You didn't drive him away, did you?"

"Don't think I could even if I wanted to."

"Stay in the open. Return before sundown. I'll be here, waiting for you. Where do you go?"

"I said I am going to Camas Creek to treat a sick girl. Did you hear me say that?"

"No, I heard the sound of bird wings. Are the ravens ready to mate?"

WolfShe stepped outside and looked around. "No. Too early for that, Ama. Here, sip broth before I leave."

"I should sort these feathers for my blanket. They act like they're attached to birds and fly all over the house by themselves."

"Spirit feathers, Ama? Maybe the woodpeckers have returned to collect them. Watch out, they're tricky," WolfShe said and leaned down to hug Ama goodbye. "They'll punch holes in your blanket."

Ama grinned but looked at something in the distance. She muttered.

WolfShe noticed how Ama's thin, silver hair followed her scalp. Her chest grew heavy. "Ama, I should stay with you today."

"No. Do your duty. Fever in children rises quicker than floodwater. Didn't you learn anything from me, WolfShe? As medicine woman, you give your life to help others. When someone calls you…you go. Your duty as healer is sacred."

"I would like to stay with you, Ama. You look weak today."

"I feel weak. Don't stay to cut camas. Bring me honeycomb. A good hive lives in the Tree of Three, three trunks grow as one, where Camas Creek joins Big Fish River. You know the place? Honeycomb will help me. Yes, that's something special to look forward to. That will lift me up. I saw a raven-shadow, heard his call, on our doorstep before dawn, when ravens cast no shadow."

WolfShe tensed. "What kind of call?"

Ama looked up from her mat by the fire pit. "Don't worry, child, my old woman aches and pains bring trick visions to my thoughts and dreams. When I try to trace them, I come to a dark, tangled wall. Water drips over moss-covered rocks. I see no image of my death, yet the feeling sinks me like a pebble in water. The pebble shimmers in pale moonlight and vanishes. A raven-shadow passes overhead. The raven flies higher, makes a shrill cry. This morning the feather-and-bone-raven walked onto our doorstep and cawed like a pup's whimper."

"Ama, it's nothing. Don't worry."

"Bring me honeycomb. You're right; change of season affects me. You'd think I would have thought of that. I worked hard before, when I was young, so the feeling would pass. Now I rest, and it sits on me."

"Ama, when I join Running Bear's longhouse, you will become the honored elder with his grandfather. Everyone will serve you. You won't be alone, ever. I don't want to leave you now, but you've commanded me."

"One day I will leave you. When I do, say prayers in my name. I taught you all I know. I will watch over you from the Land of Mists. I will search for your ancestors. Together, we will advise and protect you. Remember. Look up. I will be the brightest golden star in the northern sky. Look up to see me smile upon you."

WolfShe kissed Ama's forehead thinking, I will always look up…and smile. I will carry your teachings in my mind and you in my heart. I will train the next medicine woman as you trained me. "Ama, I will be home soon—with hon-eycomb—your favorite, to lift your spirits."

When WolfShe stepped over the pile of cedar strips, branches, and skidding feathers, she turned to look at Ama and whispered protection prayers. She gazed at Ama's long braid, a thin rope draping her shoulder. Ama rubbed her thumb across the abalone shell clasp and closed her eyes.

⁕

WolfShe carried her last image of Ama as a bless-ing and a sorrow. She wasn't there to give Ama honeycomb, her favorite, before she rose to the Land of Mists. Every cloudless night, WolfShe looked to the northern sky to see Ama twinkling.

CHAPTER NINE

Encounter

Making her way along muddy trails, WolfShe's thoughts turned to the excitement of foraging tender licorice fern to make infusions for treating measles, sore throats, and colds. She preferred the longer fronds for lining herb baskets. She made mental notes of supplies she needed for spring births. Sitka spruce bark. Wild cherry. Charcoal powder for the infant's cord. This birthing season, she would attend the women without Ama's guidance. She trained an assistant, but no one could replace her Ama.

WolfShe realized most of the tribe respected her healing skills, even if they didn't fully trust her. Some called her Wolf-Totem-healer, others…wolf-demon-protector. She laughed when a village woman saw her with Three-Legged. The woman picked up a bough of cedar and waved it to cleanse the air of her demon vision. WolfShe tried to calm her. She said he was a warm-blooded wolf with three legs. WolfShe held him by his neck mantle and called the woman over to touch him. One stare from wolf's gold eyes sent the woman screaming.

She reminded herself that at first she had feared him. She never knew how—or if—the wild would show in him.

She had watched him study children at play, his eyes tracking their every move, his nose quivering, taking in their
scent. She spoke harshly to him. He retreated. She knew
his nature-balance was delicate and fluid. She felt the
same. How much wild could be contained, she wondered,
in human or beast? She decided to visit Three-Legged in
his territory rather than call him to hers. If he did come,
he came with purpose. More than just Three-Legged, he
had become her friend, teacher, protector, and servant.
His absence during mating season had been long, but she
hoped to see him today, to caress his dark scruff, and possibly meet his mate.

WolfShe walked up-meadow, stopping at the red elderberry patch. Immature clusters of red berries weighed
down sharp-toothed leaves. The harvest would be good,
once they swelled with sunlight. The day warmed; WolfShe
slowed. She sat on a high rock to look out at the sea. A thin
layer of fog lifted from the blue water, sunlight crested
small waves, and overhead an eagle sailed on wind cur-
rents, lacing through tufts of puffy, white clouds. WolfShe
felt the eagle's joy, his freedom. She watched the bird sail
toward a mass of sticks lodged into the crevice of the tall-
est tree in sight. His mate swooped in with more sticks. A
helpmate is a good idea, WolfShe thought. Ama was right.
Running Bear's a good man. She wanted him for me, and
she was the wisest person to walk the earth. Soon I will
join Running Bear's family, and we will honor Ama at our
Union Day Ceremony.

She shouted to the eagles, "Your eggs will be safe up
in that tree that touches clouds. The Land of Mists floats
above your white heads. Tell me, do you escort the dead
into the Mists? You fly without effort; you see with preci-

sion. Do you look down and pity us poor Two-Leggeds? WolfShe watched the great eagles rise from their nest, black wings slicing the breeze, and disappear behind the mountain.

She stretched out on the warm ground and closed her eyes. Her muscles softened. She dozed. A gentle tickle on her face woke her. A bent stalk of grass touched her cheek. She jumped up, gathered her baskets, and walked the stony path uphill, looking for ripe salmonberries along the way. Many of the green, leafy canes still had pink blossoms. But WolfShe spotted some berries. Edging along the thicket, she picked them, filling a small basket, and continued up the ridge. A strange sound caught her attention. She stopped and cocked her head. She held her breath to listen. On the breeze, she caught a wavering cry. Bird call? Wolf? She couldn't tell. She trotted in the direction of the sound.

Knowing she shouldn't, she entered the black forest where branches strangled daylight. She lowered her baskets to the ground near a rotting, fern-covered log. With only her medicine bag and knife, she crept through the undergrowth, toward the sound of a birthing animal…or a dying one. She crouched behind a tree to study the terrain. She saw something quiver in the distance. She drew closer.

WolfShe spotted a human arm, flailing, a fish-belly-white arm. She crouched close to the ground, inhaling the odor of rotting wood, moss, and a vile stench she recognized. Dying animals—especially humans—can be vicious, she reminded herself. She wanted to turn and run. Let him die, she thought. Let the wolf-killer feel pain. She crept through the underbrush, drawing closer. She moved without sound, a talent she developed as a lone child. Through the dim light, she spotted his body, flailing, gasping, moaning. Pale Face is dying.

She edged closer, sweeping an arc around him to survey the injury. The wolf-killer lay maimed, the earth around him wet with blood. She spoke to him like she would speak to a small child in her native tongue. The man moaned like cooing doves. She spoke again, loudly. Pale Face tilted his head her direction, the hint of blue in his pale eyes had washed away, leaving only the reflection of gray sky and dark tree boughs. WolfShe stood still, watching. He attempted to push up on his arms. His chest collapsed onto the soft earth. His eyes rolled. He passed out.

WolfShe leaped forward to look where *metul* teeth bit above the ankle. From the smell, she knew he had endured the night in the trap. His spirit flickered and drifted up into the forest trees but sank back into his weak body and shook. Pale Face groaned; little life remained. She sat back on her haunches and watched his suffering. She spoke again. She saw a flicker of movement under his lids. His face, like sun-bleached bone, was dry and cracked. She couldn't see the extent of the injury. His blood-soaked leather pants stuck to the *metul* teeth. She slit the leather, pulling it away in strips. She inspected his swollen, purple, bloody leg.

WolfShe jumped up and ran. Dragging a heavy tree limb, breathing hard from the effort, she returned and positioned it. Lifting the thinner end, she walked the heavy branch upright using her body to steady it. She pivoted and wedged the limb between the gap in the *metul* jaws where his leg was caught. She positioned it to fall away from the body. She let the heavy branch drop. Wood cracked. Pale Face screamed. *Metul* teeth opened. She grabbed Pale Face under his arms and dragged him free. She stumbled out of reach. His body spasmed violently. She moved in and felt his neck for life-river movement. It was like a stream choked by stones.

She spoke. "You live but not long. I will try to help you."

She dashed for her medicine basket, returned, and pulled out cedar bandages and wound ointment. She cleaned the gash with dew-damp ferns. Pale Face twitched. She knew she must work fast, before he became alert…if he became alert. She felt no sympathy for the wolf-killer, nor trust, but she couldn't leave him to die. Her medicine woman training dictated to save, not slaughter…and never abandon. She felt no Four-Legged, or Two-Legged, should die this way, not even her enemy.

WolfShe swabbed death lily ointment in his mouth, cleaned the wound, packed it with salve, tied it tight with cedar bandages and secured it with her basket's leather straps. She couldn't move him. She didn't want to. She knew he might not survive. The spirits of those forest animals he had killed might bring their kind to take him in the night, lured by the smell of weakness and blood. She whispered a prayer to Great Spirit. She had followed her training. That was as much as she owed. She took out more death lily infusion and poured a generous amount into the dry corners of his mouth. She knew this would bring him relief…or death.

WolfShe gathered her things and sprinted back to the creek to wash. With her tunic still dripping wet, she bolted down the mountain trail. She thought she heard a distant howl, but it might have been the wind rushing past her ears. She reminded herself she had done what she could do as a healer, what she was obligated to do. Her hands were clean. Her mind was not.

She kept seeing Pale Face in the moment before he passed out. He looked into her eyes. She felt revulsion…

and something else. She saw his hatred as clearly as she had seen Black Snake. She couldn't spit the image away. She didn't want to feel what she felt from him, the hardness, the frenzy…the yearning. His look terrorized her.

WolfShe had no idea what the Land of Mists held for Pale Faces, or if they journeyed there at all. She hoped they had a land of their own, far, far from her people. They were so new to the world that the sun hadn't blessed them. They were creatures of the moon and night. They knew nothing of Earth Mother, much less Great Spirit. WolfShe figured at death they returned to the place where sky sucked color from their eyes and their white skin turned to ash.

Pale Face, the ill omen, came as Raven People had whispered to Ama when he first arrived…before his *metul* jaws bit wolves. When feather-and-bone raven had visited Ama before her death, WolfShe wondered, did he warn Ama that Pale Face would reappear? She longed to talk to Ama, to get her reassurance. Pale Face had cursed her with something she couldn't understand. He made her spirit quake.

CHAPTER TEN

Union Day

Running Bear smiled at WolfShe in her ceremonial clothes. He knew their union would not have happened if Ama hadn't pushed WolfShe to accept him. She encouraged him to be her daughter's friend when they were young children. Ama would invite him over to talk to WolfShe, but she would turn away, crawl into the corner, and pull her hair over her face. He thought she looked like *Dask'iya*, the kelp-haired witch from fireside stories, the one who stole children and cooked them. He was scared. He was twelve winters old and she was eight, Ama guessed. Later, he realized Ama had said things to keep other boys away. Running Bear thought WolfShe was beautiful and strange, the most fearsome girl he'd ever seen. Two years later, Ama asked him if he thought WolfShe would make a good mate. He didn't reply. He ran home. When he told his mother, she laughed.

He admired how the woven cedar-cloth skirt rippled like water when she moved. Ama had secretly worked on the ceremonial dress for several seasons while WolfShe was out gathering. She had given it to Running Bear's mother to keep until their Union Day. Running Bear regretted that

Ama hadn't lived long enough to see her daughter wear it. She had sewn circles of abalone shell on the skirt and tunic. With every movement, they caught the sunlight and shimmered silvery pink and purple. Her cape jingled with olivella shells that sang a quiet song when their conical tips touched. WolfShe had never worn such fine clothes. In fact, he had never seen any woman of their tribe dressed so well. Running Bear felt proud…and relieved. He worried WolfShe would never accept him.

His family gifted WolfShe a sea-otter tooth etched with a thin black line and an abalone shell inlaid cedar box—usually reserved for an elder of great wisdom—their way of showing respect. Several tribes walked long distances to celebrate their union. Not in Running Bear's memory had a potlatch of such magnitude taken place. And this, he knew, was due to her…not him. This woman, spat from the sea onto a high mountain, who survived in the wild until Ama found her, had earned respect, even without ancestors to claim her. Now, many spoke of her as the next *shaman*. They said she'd driven Pale Face, the trapper of Wolf People, from their land and had sent his spirit to Great Spirit's dungeon. But they didn't know, as Running Bear did, that WolfShe had tried to save her enemy, something Running Bear could not understand and would never speak of.

When Running Bear looked at WolfShe, he saw a girl who'd grown into a woman. Everything about her spoke of power, her thick black hair, sparkling night eyes, and muscular strength that even young braves longed for. Running Bear couldn't hide his admiration, especially today at their union ceremony, when his mate would be blessed by the tribes, acknowledged for her healing skills and bravery, and become his…and his alone.

If only Ama could share this day, he thought. He knew WolfShe had hoped, more than anything, to make Ama happy. She had told Running Bear the greatest joy for Ama, after seeing her become medicine woman, would have been to see her join with him. Ama had dreamed of their union, even when WolfShe rejected the idea. Running Bear chose Ama to be the honored guest at their potlatch, her place marked by a special ceremonial blanket where her spirit would sit.

❧

AMA'S DEATH HAD BEEN HARD ON WOLFSHE. SHE CHOSE to remain alone after Ama departed, wanting to weave ritual baskets the way Ama had taught her to heal sorrow. Running Bear visited her every day, pleading for her to stay with his family at their longhouse. He told her she shouldn't stay alone, everyone worried for her safety, but WolfShe held firm. She wanted to grieve in Ama's home. She reminded Running Bear she lived in the cabin of the greatest medicine woman who had ever lived, and it was protected by her prayers. No evil could enter. She wanted time to feel the love in everything Ama had touched, to recall Ama's words, to remember her stories, to be silent, to listen, and to offer prayers. She wanted to pay respect to the woman who saved her, tamed her, gave her a home, the only person who had believed in her—the person who loved her after her family perished in the Great Flood.

Running Bear respected WolfShe's way. He brought her firewood and food every day until the elder council demanded she move in closer, for her own safety. When the council offered her a cabin adjoining the healing longhouse in Green Valley Village, Running Bear's village, WolfShe accepted. But she continued to prepare medicines at Ama's longhouse. Only Running Bear understood why she walked every sunrise to Ama's cabin. For Three-Legged.

⸺∽∾∽⸺

RUNNING BEAR WATCHED PEOPLE GATHER IN THE LONGhouse for their union, remembering the evening the shaman from Gull Rock Island showed up seeking the healer-girl WolfShe. A brave led him to Running Bear's longhouse where the family offered him a sleeping mat for the night. When Running Bear and the shaman arrived the next morning at Ama's cabin, they found WolfShe preparing poultices. Running Bear sat and listened to them exchange information.

The shaman told her of an illness that had come to Gull Rock from the mainland. Traders brought it, the man said. Pale Face traders, the ones who bartered for smoked salmon and beads. They arrived with a dead man in their canoe. The other two dragged his body out, tossed it onto the sand, and rowed away. The body was covered with red, putrid sores. The fishermen, watching from the trees, waited until the canoe was out of sight and pulled the body away from the water, built a mound of sticks and grasses, and burned it. They fell ill with the same oozing sore disease. Then their families.

He implored WolfShe to teach him her methods, saying his remedies had not worked on the fisherman's family. No one remained on that end of the island but him. For seven sunrises he stayed alone, waiting. No sores appeared on his body. No illness came. In a cleansing sweat, he received this message: *Seek the healer spared in the Great Flood.*

He recounted how he treated the sores, with boiled sword-fern poultices, but the sores grew angrier and spread. Fever and sweats spread a pale-yellow sap that erupted in red sores. The ill died quickly. He wondered if greasing his hands with elk fat had saved him, but WolfShe didn't know why it would. She questioned his belief that illness enters through the skull. She explained why she thought through the gut.

Illness travels the body like we travel footpaths, she said. Many trails. You have to stop it where it begins. I believe burning sores erupt through the skin from poison in the gut. Hemlock bark tea helps. She advised him to burn cedar boughs day and night to keep evil spirits and rodents away and to offer the patient only boiled salmon water. When the stomach sleeps, broth is best.

He showed WolfShe the deer leather gloves he wore, a gift from his shaman, recounting that once his teacher had gotten very sick from collecting stinging nettle, almost died. His teacher told him gloves keep demons out of the body and wearing a mask of pungent smelling herbs scares them. Demons blow their breath on you when you sleep. You don't wake from the oozing sore illness. The Gull Rock tribe believed demon breath traveled from the mainland over the sea like fog, killing the pale-faced trader and then the fishermen on the beach.

WolfShe invited the healer to stay for two sunrises. They worked sunup to sundown, making decoctions for him to take back and for her to store. When he left, she gave him a special herbal ointment to rub on his hands before putting on gloves, saying, what good are we healers, if we die of illness?

_⸎_

AFTER THAT VISIT RUNNING BEAR REALIZED WOLFSHE HAD changed. She no longer roamed alone—she let him know where she would be without being asked—and she worked long hours into the night preparing medicines to treat an outbreak of oozing sore disease. He wanted this day, their Union Day, to acknowledge the gift his tribe had received in WolfShe. Ama departed for the Land of Mists making WolfShe their only medicine woman, but today she would be honored as the tribe's shaman. Running Bear understood Ama's medicine ways had not ended. Her vision had become real. She had promised him three harvests back that WolfShe would become his mate. Today he would honor Ama and WolfShe with his sacred dance: for his chosen mate, for the tribe's chosen shaman, and for the great healer and wise woman who helped birth and heal so many.

_⸎_

"WOLFSHE," RUNNING BEAR SAID AS SHE WALKED UP TO the potlatch, "The elders bless us, our family, your ancestors, our tribe, in the eyes of Great Spirit today—in _your_ honor—at our Union Day Ceremony. They will announce something Ama would be very happy to hear. The council has named you, Medicine Woman of Wolf Totem, our new Shaman."

WolfShe pursed her lips and swallowed hard. "Running Bear, I wish Ama could be here. She taught me everything. The honor is all hers. I don't _feel_ like a shaman. I lack the wisdom."

"The council has spoken. Ama shares your honor and will be at our ceremony in spirit. I placed an honorary mat for her. The ceremony starts with the Jumping Dance. Then braves and I dance the Thunderbird Dance outside on the roof. Our dance will crack the sky for Ama. She will see her daughter blessed as our new shaman. If you look closely, you'll see me, but you might not recognize me. The braves wear headdresses and black shawls that cover our bodies. Come, look at my headdress," Running Bear said, leading WolfShe into the longhouse.

"White eagle feathers, Running Bear, for you to wear?"

"Yes, sacred, very powerful. For you, too. Braves will dance; drummers will create thunder, and our wooden whistles will split the air. The spirit world will open. Shaman WolfShe, you will visit the spirit world and bring us blessings from the ancestors."

"Will Great Spirit descend like an eagle and bring Ama?"

"I don't have the sight, you do. Chief Lightning Bolt will bless you with this sacred headdress decorated with white eagle feathers and beads," Running Bear said and lifted the headdress from its stand. "He'll place the headdress on you after the dance, the greatest honor a chief can give, and declare you *shaman*. This brings you great power to help people when their spirits are weak. Women chant, so you journey safely and return to us with guidance and blessings. The greatest honor for you, WolfShe…and on our Union Day. Do you understand? A ceremony like this hasn't been performed since my grandfather's childhood."

WolfShe looked at Running Bear with a grin. "Do I understand? Which part? The ceremony…or our union?"

"The ceremony is to honor you," Running Bear said with a smile. "I think you understand that better than I do. The union, later tonight, when we join as mates for life, I understand better than you."

WolfShe rubbed her cheek against his. "The women I've helped birthing told me what to expect."

Running Bear wrapped his arms around WolfShe and held her close. "We become one, and I serve you for life."

"Serve me?"

"Yes. Great Spirit commanded the sea to spit you out and saved you from dying in the Great Flood…for a reason. Today I found a carving I'd made years ago. Missing objects that appear on a day like this have special meaning. I'm going to complete it for you as a protection."

"I have something for you too," she said and picked up a bundle from the floor and handed it to Running Bear.

"A blanket? You made it?"

"Yes. Woodpecker feathers, dog hair, and cattail fluff stuffing covered with the softest cedar bark cloth ever… beaten, by me. See the plaid design? Ama taught me that. Plus, it's blessed to repel bad dreams and to keep you safe, always."

"Bad dreams? How could I have a bad dream with you next to me?"

"Well, bad dreams come to me. I hope they leave when I'm next to you."

Running Bear studied WolfShe's dark eyes. He saw raven wings darken a moonlit lake where something coiled in shadow. He stumbled backward and saw a raven cross the longhouse entrance, at night. "What dreams, WolfShe?" he demanded.

"Pale Face…he haunts me. Let's not talk of this now."

"WolfShe, Pale Face died. We hunted for him. We found nothing. Animals finished him. We saw many animal tracks that followed his blood. Signs of a struggle ended with nothing."

"You've never told me."

"I tried. Remember, you sent me away? I saw stains on your tunic, I thought from berries. When I held you close, I smelled blood. At dawn, I took braves to hunt the woods. We found the *metul* trap, half buried, with pieces of bloody leather stuck to it. A swath of crushed ferns had blood stains on the fronds. Animal tracks—wolf, coyote, and cougar—crisscrossed the area. Nothing was left of him. Nothing. If Cougar People dragged him away, they didn't bother to bury the body to eat later. They had their meal."

"I did everything I could, Running Bear, to ease his suffering," WolfShe confessed, tears forming in her eyes.

"You tried to save him? Why? WolfShe, even a healer must destroy at times. He would have killed you like he killed wolves. I'm glad his trap snared him. I'm glad he was eaten; otherwise, he would have hunted you. Pale Face had no reverence for Great Spirit's children, four-legged, or two. Great Spirit sent him to Shadow Fog, cleansed Earth Mother of him."

"What if…he lives?"

"How could he after losing so much blood? He would have dragged that leg like a useless stump of wood, making an easy track to follow, and a short one. Only leaving by canoe could have saved him, but first he'd have to reach water, impossible with an injury like that."

"In my dreams, he is in a canoe…looking for me."

Running Bear took WolfShe by the shoulders in a firm hold and shook her. "I will protect you. Have no fear of a Pale Face ghost. He died a cruel death by his own doing. If his spirit haunts you, the Thunderbird Dance will destroy it. You did what no one would have done…you tried to save your enemy. You should have let him rot! He deserved nothing better. Touching him allowed his spirit to cling to you. That's why you see him in dreams. We'll hold a special sweat lodge in your honor as our new shaman, one for women, one for braves. That will cleanse the memory of him from you and from our land. No one knows you tried to save him. No one should. Do not tell anyone, WolfShe. They will see it as weakness. The braves and I said he had stepped into his own trap and animals finished him. That is what people believe. That is what happened."

"Running Bear, his eyes, his putrid smell, I can't forget. In my dreams I see him looking at me. He's wounded. Then he glides across slow-moving water, mist rises from the surface, and he turns back to come for me."

"Then?"

"He disappears in fog. I wake shaking, cold sweat clinging to my hair."

"Demons travel in fog. His spirit attached to you because you were the last human eyes he saw before he died. He lives only in your fear."

"I've held ceremony myself many times. Nothing has worked."

"Now you'll do it with the tribe's help. No phantom can stand up to that."

WolfShe's fear made Running Bear's chest tighten. He shook the image away. He smiled and tickled her ribs.

"Running Bear!"

"For first-night union, mother decorated the healing cabin for us, so we can be alone. At the crescent moon, we'll move into my family's longhouse."

Running Bear's mother had left food in the cabin, salmonberry cakes and fish eggs, for their first night and had set aside enough for many nights after. She informed her son the eggs would make WolfShe fertile, so she could bear many children. When he whispered those words to WolfShe, she tilted her head and whispered, "Only two—one girl, one boy—since I have many shaman-healer duties."

Running Bear smiled and agreed. He and several braves had spent much of the summer working on a new whaling canoe big enough for twelve men, twelve harpoons, and many nets. They had dragged the huge trunk from the north woods. The final layer of grease took three days to cure, but now it was seaworthy and ready for whaling season. But elk were on the move, and he intended to hunt before the rains came. He knew his mother hoped for a grandchild from first-union night. He preferred more time, so he and WolfShe could learn each other's ways.

⁂

CHIEF LIGHTNING BOLT SIGNALED. THE CEREMONY began. WolfShe took her seat with the women, Running Bear with the men. Two young girls walked through the crowd carrying smoldering cedar incense wands while the chief chanted. With upturned prayer hands, the crowd whisked the smoke around their faces.

Running Bear's father stepped forward to address the gathering and motioned Running Bear and WolfShe to join him. He announced that his son, Running Bear, chose WolfShe for his life mate: WolfShe, the adopted daughter of Medicine Woman of Raven Totem. Ama would join the ceremony in spirit to bless them with her Raven Totem ancestors as his family blessed them with their Bear Totem ancestors. A rare person, he pointed out, enjoys protection from three totems. "WolfShe came to us from mystery. We know nothing of her life before the Great Flood. She learned medicine craft from Ama and heals our community. She protects Wolf People. She faced the pale-faced demon and drove him from our land." Yips of tribute interrupted the elder's words. Running Bear's father silenced the crowd with a hand wave. He continued, "We celebrate, remember, and honor our loved ones on this special Union Day—those here and those in spirit—first with Jumping Dance and then Thunderbird Dance in the couple's honor."

Chief Lightning Bolt stepped up, joined by braves wearing red, black, and white woodpecker feather headbands. Drummers beat a rhythm as they danced while the chief recounted a story.

"Long, long ago, Earthquake ran along the beach. His heavy feet cracked the ground. Ocean poured in. People ran to the mountaintop to drive Earthquake away, to calm him, so he would leave the villages in peace, but many villages slipped into the cracks. Few lived, but those that did were strong. From those survivors, Great Spirit chose his new people. For a long time, no big shake came because tribes offered Jumping Dance prayers to please Great Spirit and Earth Mother. Today we offer Jumping Dance prayers to show our respect on this special day. We ask Great Spirit to allow Great Flood and Earthquake peaceful sleep, to protect our land and people, and to allow our medicine woman to heal our sick and keep evil spirits away. We proclaim WolfShe our shaman and bless her with Thunderbird Dance in honor of her work with Ama, Medicine Woman of Raven Totem, who dances with us in spirit."

Chief Lightning Bolt motioned a boy to come forward who was holding a headband of woodpecker feathers on his outstretched palms. The dark feathers, arranged in pairs, stood along an elk leather band, white spots at the top, a small crest of bright red center front. He placed the woodpecker headband low on WolfShe's forehead. The old man's voice sang a blessing chant that seemed to rumble along the mountain rims, dip into clear cold streams, and grow like spring shoots awakening from winter-slumber earth. Everyone swayed with the power.

Running Bear stood with WolfShe at his side. His father joined their hands and bound them with a length of elk hide decorated with abalone shell discs and colored glass beads. He said, "Together you serve Great Spirit and our people. Be fruitful and be blessed." He placed the eagle feather headdress on his son. Then he ordered the boy to bring out another eagle feather headdress. He placed it on WolfShe's head, above the woodpecker headband, saying, "These eagle feathers will protect you in your work. Use the power and strength of the eagle to fly high to commune with the ancestors, to bring back healing for our people, and to defeat demons. WolfShe, wear these headdresses as signs of our respect."

Running Bear's father motioned Running Bear to speak. Running Bear looked at WolfShe, and then turned to address the gathering.

"Many worked long and hard to make a fine long-long rope. Those who lived before without long-long ropes perished. With one, we can always find our way home. A long-long rope of hope saved WolfShe, something her father taught us with his bravery. With this cedar long-long rope, your people, WolfShe, live in our children. And our children will weave long-long ropes in your father's memory and to honor your mother and sister and all your ancestors. This I promise you. They are not forgotten."

WolfShe covered her eyes with her hand to hide tears flowing like spring-melt down her tunic. Successive rapid drumbeats split the air and cracked the sky. Chants filled the house, bouncing off the wood boards, draping them all like a warm feather blanket. WolfShe remained rigid, unable to look up until Running Bear nudged her when a line of braves entered supporting a thick cedar rope held high above their heads. They paraded around the gathering to stop where Running Bear and WolfShe stood. The braves lowered the rope to the ground and stepped away.

Running Bear said, "With this long-long rope we honor your family and the many lost in the Great Flood. They are not forgotten."

The chief shouted for the dancers. Seven men and women in woodpecker headbands lifted their knees high, held the beat mid-air, and stomped the earth to the drums' rhythm while women chanted. After several rounds, Chief Lightning Bolt waved cedar incense and asked the gathering to exit the longhouse to watch the Thunderbird Dance on the roof.

Running Bear put on his eagle feather headdress and black shawl to join the braves on the roof. By the time WolfShe took her place outside, she couldn't recognize which dancer was Running Bear. They pounded the thick cedar planks with quick moving steps. Drummers below beat thunder. Clouds overhead broke. Moonlight shone silver on the white-tipped eagle feathers. Women and men blew wooden whistles to rip a hole in the sky, to open the spirit world.

WolfShe swayed. Running Bear looked down at her. She teetered. His mother rushed to steady her, but WolfShe fell against the chief, her eyes rolled back. Running Bear saw slivers of moonlight pierce her like small arrows. She groaned. He jumped to the ground to grab her.

Chief Lightning Bolt waved people back, shouting, "Medicine Woman had a vision. Give her air. In two sunrises she will tell us her message. Now, go inside."

WolfShe woke in Running Bear's arms, disoriented and stunned. He lifted her upright. She swayed in his embrace. She gulped crisp night air. She revived and blinked, whispering, "Do we feast now, Running Bear? We must lead the people."

Running Bear and WolfShe led the procession into the hall and received the first bite of blessed food, as the honored guests, before the others. His mother raised WolfShe's hand aloft and led the women in a fertility prayer for the young couple. Running Bear saw WolfShe's downturned eyes, closed tight. She didn't look up to meet the women's gaze. Running Bear knew her tears were not related to childbearing. She had seen something. What, she didn't say.

CHAPTER ELEVEN

Three-Legged

Cold, lashing rain beat the cedar boards of the family longhouse day and night. Storms roared in and showed no signs of easing up. North winds blew through the cracks, making a whistling noise that kept everyone up at night. Water ditches caught rain from the roof and ran like streams away from the house. WolfShe tired of inside communal life. She organized her medicine baskets, checked her dried herbs and berries to make sure they weren't molding, and prepared more cedar bandages, longing to roam free.

Cold air and rain brought wet lung illness. WolfShe knew it wouldn't be long before she would have little time to think—and much less to dream—of roaming. At first, few people came for help, but as winter grew harsher more fell ill. WolfShe made infusions and heating poultices to deliver to the ill who stayed in their own homes. She hoped to keep the illness from spreading by isolating the very sick in the healing house. The council had used the healing house for storing food supplies in the summer and fall, but as wet lung sickness spread, WolfShe claimed it for her patients. She and her assistant worked hard to keep fires going, to steam herbs, and to make medicine teas. She taught her assistant the massage to break up water in the lungs. With each recovery, word spread of WolfShe Medicine Woman's talent. Neighboring villages sent messengers begging her for help. WolfShe never refused but regretted she hadn't trained more assistants.

One day a desperate message came from the village on the far side of Wolf Fang Mountain: *many ill, come help*. WolfShe knew the trek would be difficult—icy winds, slippery ground, a steep mountain climb—but she felt confident she could complete the trek in one day if she didn't stop to rest. Since wet lung had come to Green Valley Village early, most of the ill had recovered, except for an elder woman, one of Ama's cousins, who was still weak. WolfShe ordered her assistant to care for her as she prepared to leave. She organized two braves to go with her and Running Bear to Wolf Fang to carry supplies. She hoped she would be able to return before the new moon.

The trek to Wolf Fang exhausted them. Without stopping to rest, they arrived after last light. The way was slippery; the wind howled. An elder greeted them and showed them to the communal longhouse where they slept with two other families. To WolfShe's surprise, the council had dedicated a longhouse to the sick since so many suffered from wet lung.

WolfShe, Running Bear, and the two braves unrolled their mats in the longhouse. But WolfShe decided she should sleep in the healing house, in a far corner, to better administer to her patients in the night. The elder woman who had been helping was exhausted and needed to return home. When Running Bear left her at the entrance to the healing house, he said, "Try to sleep. You must be tired after the journey. I will come in the morning to say goodbye."

WolfShe discovered a new helper, an elderly grandmother, who had come saying the illness would not affect her, and if it did, she was ready for the Land of Mists. WolfShe liked the old woman. She worked hard and had healing knowledge, she said, because she had raised many children. WolfShe instructed her to administer medicine tea she had prepared and to apply warm chest compresses using moist medicine mats with warm rocks placed on top. When they had prepared all the remedies for the night, making sure each person had enough blankets, WolfShe drank broth the old woman offered her and fell into a deep sleep. She woke when she heard Running Bear's familiar sound, an owl hoot repeated three times. She stepped outside into gray light and cold air.

"I will send a message for you to return for me, Running Bear. Take care of grandfather and the family. I will miss your warm body next to mine." She rubbed cheeks with Running Bear and smiled. She felt that pull from his heart to hers, the cedar rope that secured her in his world and drew her closer and closer until her skin tingled. She smiled. "I will teach more assistants to treat wet lung, so I can stay at home with you. For now, safe journey."

⸎

WolfShe ordered more blankets from the villagers; requested mushroom, bulb, and fish broths be prepared for meals; and began teaching healing craft to two young volunteers—decoctions, poultices, herbal teas and steams, and body manipulation. She found her apprentices eager, quick learners. WolfShe felt good. These villagers looked at her with respect…untinged by fear, like some back home. She assumed they hadn't heard the story of her beginning.

She found that comforting. To always be *the-woman-spit-out-from-the-sea* made her feel as if she were something other than who she was. These people of Wolf Fang didn't whisper about a wolf that followed her, or a time when she was raised by wolves.

Her thoughts drifted to Three-Legged. She had not seen him before she left. She had not felt his *think-speak*. She hoped wolf could feel her protection prayers for him and his pack to find warmth and safety in this foul weather.

WolfShe immersed herself in the work she knew, the work she loved: healing the sick. The longhouse had seen many ill arrive and many depart, cured. Her reputation increased with every success. News spread. She had thought her stay would be short, but two full moons had come and gone. It seemed to her every sick person in the mountains had been brought to her.

A traveler showed up asking for refuge from the cold. He was exhausted from his trek. A villager escorted him to the healing house, assuming he was ill. WolfShe quickly realized he only suffered from exposure and hunger, not wet lung. She had a mat prepared for him but warned him to stay away from the ill and to keep to the back corner and not touch any medicine supplies. She fed him, placed hot rocks at his feet, and covered him with blankets while she listened to him describe an illness he had heard of that made his blood run cold. He called it *oozing sore.*

"I traveled for two days from my village. I live across from the mainland on Eagle's Perch Island. My grand-mother lives there with me. She has wet lung. I promised her I would find help when our herbs proved useless. I left my family and planned to canoe across the strait.

But I stopped at a small island when the winds came up. There coastal villagers spoke of a medicine woman working in Wolf Fang Village, the one who had survived the Great Flood. They said she captured strong healing spirits from the air when Great Spirit tossed her onto the mountain during the flood. They work with her. Are you that medicine woman?"

"I am a medicine woman, the one who survived the Great Flood. I live in Green Valley. My Ama, the greatest Medicine Woman of Raven Totem, adopted me and taught me her craft. I carry on her work. I do not capture healing spirits. That is idle talk. I work with healing potions."

"But you have magic? You are a great shaman. Everyone says so."

"No magic. For spells and incantations, go elsewhere. I understand plants and trees and natural things Great Spirit has given us for healing. That is all. I do have great success treating wet lung and other illnesses with herbs."

"Can you treat an oozing sore?"

"Infection? Harpoon wound? Animal bite? Yes. These are common. I have many remedies."

"No, the disease that kills even the strongest warrior, the best whaler. When it comes, you feel sore throat, water-burn eyes, pain, heat in the body. Then the demons arrive. Red skin explodes in sores that ooze on the face, hands, arms, all over. The sore runs pale yellow sap that grows more sores. Cold wind blows inside, then blazing sun cooks. The head and stomach quiver. Death creeps closer. Demons drag you away in the night. The dead body looks so ugly even your kin won't come close. They say the demons leave this promise: *Anyone who helps you will join you.* People are afraid to handle the dead, to give them proper ceremony.

Across the water, rumors spread that whole villages on the mainland have died from this demon sore disease. Nothing has stopped the evil."

WolfShe felt her breath shorten. "Have you seen it?"

"No. I wouldn't be here to tell you if I had. But people say pale-skinned traders and trappers bring the demons from their world where the sun doesn't shine."

"Trappers? Wolf trappers?"

"Wolf, beaver, sea otters, fur seals, mink, wild cats, many animals. They kill for pelts, especially wolves. They're a curse. Are there pale trappers here on this island?"

"There was one, but I thought he had left."

"I had never seen one until two moons ago when I saw two pale-skinned men rowing near a small outer island west of Eagle's Perch. One had hair like dried weeds, yellow and matted. The other had red-brown hair like cedar bark."

"They travel together in one canoe?"

"No, not when I saw them. Two canoes," the man said and slumped onto his mat. "Can I have more broth?"

"Cedar-hair trapper. Where is he now?" WolfShe said and motioned for an apprentice to fetch broth for the man.

"I don't know."

WolfShe shook. She slumped forward. Air rushed from her chest in a loud sigh. Her vision wavered; her hands went cold and numb. She sucked in a deep, noisy gulp of air that caught in her throat. She coughed.

"What is it, Medicine Woman, a vision? A demon?"

She faltered. "No. I am very tired. I've been awake for nights treating my patients, with only short naps in the day. Let me prepare a medicine basket for your grandmother. You must leave with morning light. I'm sorry I cannot go with you to treat her, but I will say prayers and give you all the medicines I use. She will survive this illness. Finish your broth and sleep."

"Someday I will look for you in your village of Green Valley. Thank you for the medicines. My grandmother wanted you to have this in exchange." The man handed her a finely etched sea-lion tooth attached to a leather sinew. "Grandmother said this will help you. It once belonged to a great shaman. Wear it for protection."

"A very generous gift. I am honored. May Great Spirit bring your grandmother many seasons of good health. Send news of pale-faced trappers, if you can. I met a pale-faced trapper once. Wolf People fear them."

"I fear them; so should you. Grandmother said she saw you in a vision. She knew your teacher, Ama, the respected Medicine Woman of Raven Totem."

"She did?"

"Grandmother said you need protection. Ama told her in a dream. Grandmother gave the strongest gift she owned to ward off evil."

WolfShe tipped her head in silent acknowledgment, fighting back tears, and walked to the back of the healing house where supplies were kept. She prepared the medicine basket. The man's news scared her: oozing sore disease, cedar-hair Pale Face. Running Bear had convinced her the trapper had died and had been eaten by his enemies in the forest, yet she had felt in the depth of her he had not. She had tried to convince herself of Running Bear's words, but a lingering feeling like a dim candle flame wavering in the breeze made her feel he had survived…because of her medicine, because of her skills. She had saved her enemy, the enemy of her people, the enemy of Wolf People. Now she feared her healing power would bring to her door the very thing she most dreaded. Pale Face.

She felt her world shrink around her, choke her. Her throat grew dry and tight. Cold sweat beads dappled her forehead; bitterness stung her eyes. *What have I done? What do I do now?* She struggled to toss away her fear, wishing she could lie in Running Bear's warm arms and be safe. But she could not. She immersed herself in work and fought the fear that wrenched her stomach.

Many nights passed. She heard from a great distance a miserable howl. *Three-Legged!* She tried to *think-travel* her thoughts through the cold rain, darkness, and dense woods. She could see nothing. She tried to *think-speak* with him but got no reply. *Have I imagined his howl? Is it the wind over the peaks?* She sat very still and strained to listen. She heard nothing except deep snores, the crackling of burning wood, and the low whispers of her two helpers before they fell asleep.

WolfShe finished medicine baskets for her elderly grandmother assistant, her two apprentices, and a small one for herself. She had instructed her apprentices how to care for the remaining patients, all nearly healed, saying she must return to her home at dawn and for them to run the healing house without her. She felt good about what she and her helpers had accomplished. Two mothers had returned to their children, a grandfather had ambled home, several fishermen had grown strong enough to prepare winter nets, and two small children—her greatest worry—played and laughed again. The remaining two patients needed more rest. Then the healing house would be empty.

WolfShe lay down to sleep, hoping to dream her family totem, to find someone who had known her family just as one of Ama's old friends had found her. Suddenly it seemed possible. Somewhere an elder in the islands would know of them, she felt sure. WolfShe felt connected to Ama in the Land of Mists, carrying on her work, but now she needed Ama in front of her, to counsel her. She implored Great Spirit to gift her a vision of Ama, but she received no such vision; instead her mind cracked open like a fragile robin egg.

She could no longer bury the vision she had seen on Union Day, the vision she denied, the vision that haunted her. Not a beautiful vision of Ama, as she had hoped, but instead something that scared her into silence. When the chief had asked her two days later to relate what she had seen, she denied having had a vision. But she had. She saw Pale Face, alive, hunting her, his narrow eyes tracking her footprints, his head raised to her scent, and she heard Ama scream. WolfShe's spirit sunk to the depths of the obsidian lake where Black Snake uncoiled, where he wrapped around her and bound her to his darkness. She spoke of this to no one.

WolfShe heard something outside. She reached under the sleeping mat for her knife and eased it out. She studied the longhouse entrance. She jerked. Gold eyes, reflecting the fire's orange flames, eased past the elk hide curtain. Sniffing the air, walking silently, Three-Legged came over and nudged WolfShe with his long, cold muzzle. He licked her face.

You, my friend, she *thought-spoke.* I wondered if you'd forgotten me. I've missed you, she said rubbing his thick gray fur. I never expected to meet you like this. It's not safe for you here. Her thoughts ran through his long coat and lodged in his tired muscles. Rest now. The wolf stretched out next to her. She pulled a blanket over them and descended into a peaceful sleep, listening to his heartbeat.

When WolfShe woke before morning light, she reached over to rub her wolf. Her eyes jerked wide open. Wolf? She jumped up and checked the longhouse. She rushed back to where they had lain and felt the mat. No smell. No fur. No warmth. WolfShe shivered like morning frost had fanned her spine. Spirit, or flesh wolf? Who visited me in the dark? He seemed so real—thick fur, warm body, woodsy smell of moss, rotting cedar, and rich earth, soft breathing, strong heartbeat. What does wolf want?

She shook off the sensation and tried to tame her thoughts running like elk from a fire. She wrapped her shawl around her shoulders, hoisted her empty medicine baskets on her back, and stepped out into pale purple dawn to see villagers gathered to thank her with gifts and prayers. She figured her assistants must have spread the word. She had wanted to leave quietly, to sneak away. She shied away from tributes. The villagers blessed her, touching her with feathers, and presented gifts, too many and too heavy to carry. She told her assistants to store them in the longhouse until she returned. She promised when winter lifts to see them again, sooner if needed, but she had left them with well-trained assistants.

When she hugged her aides goodbye, WolfShe felt sorry to leave them. They had become sisters. She waved farewell and walked away in crisp, cold, light. A good day for walking, she thought, and then realized she had not kept her promise to Running Bear. She had meant to send him a message to escort her home, but the traveler's tale of oozing sore disease and the vision of her wolf made her feel an urgency she couldn't dispel, not even in cold sunshine.

She walked along, lost in thought, but heard passersby whisper: Is that the girl who survived the Great Flood? They say she heals by pulling demons off the sick. Wolves follow her. She made a pale-faced trader vanish, sent him to the Land of Shadow Fog. Sorceress, Demon Slayer, Healer, Wolf-Totem Girl, Medicine Woman: many names they spoke under their breath, just loud enough for WolfShe to hear. An old man warned the idle gossipers that wagging tongues bind them to her. He said the medicine woman avenges any wrong done to her and her wolf—for any reason, especially a slight from the wagging tongues of ignorant villagers. They quickly trotted away.

She thought, How they run from me like I'm stinging nettle but rush back with open arms when their loved ones are healed. I prefer the company of wolves. Yes, she smiled under her shawl, I travel with a wolf. No, he is not my totem. I have no totem. I have no people. I healed him, made him strong again. He thanks me with friendship. At times he's flesh, at times spirit. We are bound. My name is WolfShe.

She followed the dirt path, leaving the chattering villagers behind, and followed the river east. I wish Three-Legged were here, she thought. His soft breathing and jagged gait comfort me. She understood moving to Green Valley Village meant the wildness she shared with wolf had tamed in her. She had grown up, living with Running Bear's family in their longhouse, performing medicine duties, being a mate. She wanted family and companionship…but wild blood warmed her veins. She yearned to run with her wolf in the forest, a chill breeze in her hair, to scan the darkness for the first star, to see silver droplets on the meadow at dawn, to bathe in cold stream water, to be free like her wolf.

WolfShe entered Forbidden Trees, the shortest distance home, and the least advisable. Shafts of light cut the forest in dark-light ribbons that fooled the eye. Moss glowed green against orange-brown decaying cedar trees knocked down long ago, now used as homes for young trees to sprout. She inhaled the familiar odor of damp earth and cedar and watched eagles fly high overhead, carving circles in the broken morning sky. WolfShe felt wary. She stopped to rest and ate roasted bulbs a villager had given her. Wrapping her shawl close, she fell asleep on a bed of cedar needles.

When she woke, she saw the sun had sunk down the trees, melting liquid gold on small waves in the distant sea. The air chilled quickly. Short-day darkness comes fast. She realized she must stay in the forest for the night. She remembered the perfect place, where three large boulders formed a stone shelter. She had slept there often as a child. As an adult she had visited, always surprised at the narrowness of the crevice. She knew what once looked huge would now hug her when she crawled in. As a child she believed water had shaped the rocks and put the flat one on top of the two uprights to make a safe place for her. Now, as an adult in the woods, she believed the same. She headed toward her special place to take refuge for the night.

The uphill climb slowed her pace. Even in fading light, she knew every turn, every rock on the trail. Her memory of the hiding place had never left her. When she reached the dense clump of cedar trees, she picked her way around their massive, hairy trunks with ease. She felt her way up the boulders until she came to the ledge. She hoisted her baskets, then her body, up. She felt her way to the crevice. She dropped her baskets first. They hit the flat shelf below;

no animal growled. She shimmied down the narrow crack, scraping on the rough rock. It seemed only a moonrise ago that she had hidden there as a young girl. She instantly felt at home. She pulled out the feather blanket a villager gifted her, wrapped her shawl close, and stretched out in the black cavern. Her eyes closed to the world of stone and trees and opened to the world of dreams.

WolfShe felt a sharp whack on her back. The ground rumbled and groaned like an animal. Small rocks pinged down the hill followed by large stones. Treetops swayed, branches cracked, and trunks shattered into jagged golden shards. Green needles littered the damp earth. Air whipping the mountain face roared through the rock crevice. The world fell silent. Then tree, rock, water, wind, earth, star, plant, and animal swirled in circles, collided, and split into a million little pieces that rushed to a black opening. Only the North Star remained constant. Only that small wedge of sky stood still. WolfShe reached up, tried to grab the star…but paws pulled her down.

WolfShe woke with a start. She sat up and banged her forehead into rock. The impact made her wince and whimper. A small trickle of blood slid down her face. She heard breathing. She inhaled a familiar, pungent odor: "Three-Legged?" Her voice bumped across the rough rock wall and whispered back to her: *Three-Legged.*

"I had a dream. But here you are. You travel like a ghost." The wolf lowered his head and stretched out beside her. She rubbed his fur. "We will never part. I recognize you now. You *are* my childhood. We played like pups. When I saw that trap, it broke my heart to see a wolf suffer, yet I didn't recognize you. Later, when you came to Ama's, I realized you came for a purpose, but I didn't know what.

   D Y A N   D U B O I S

But tonight…I see clearly. Great Spirit awakened me. You have been with me all along."

WolfShe rubbed the soft fur between Three-Legged's ears. He licked her arm. She ran her finger down his long muzzle to his damp nose tip. "Seeing you here, in the cave of my childhood, is no chance meeting. You come with a warning, don't you? Speak." The wolf snorted and shifted position. "Have we lost *think-speak*? Have too many seasons passed? Do you not talk to me because I've grown older? Because I became a mate? You have traveled far, maybe too far away from me. I feel your heart beating, strong and even. I smell the journey caught in your fur, from dried summer grass to cool wind, to wet earth full of ferns and moss. Yet something else clings to you. What is it? Tell me." Wolf lifted his head for a moment, his gold eyes shining in the darkness. His flank rose and fell against her ribs with his breath. WolfShe nestled closer. They slept.

A shaft of bright light pierced the cave opening, bouncing off rock crystals in the wall to form tiny stars. WolfShe blinked. She reached for her wolf. She waved her hands in large circles. She was alone. "Why do you appear like a ghost, smell like earth, turn to vapor, and disappear?" she hissed. She scooped up her shawl. Something tickled her chin. She picked several dark gray hairs from the shawl's weave. No phantom sheds, she sighed.

CHAPTER TWELVE

Going Home

—◦∿◦—

Running Bear ran to meet WolfShe when he spotted her on the trail to Green Valley. He grabbed her and held her close. The chill of the morning melted with his heat.

"You didn't send word. I wanted to come for you. Your escorts?"

"I traveled alone, two sunrises."

"You slept alone? Did something drive you away?

"Yes. Missing you," WolfShe said with a smile. "Plus, the ill recovered. My work was done."

Running Bear's raised brow furrowed. "WolfShe, that was not our agreement. Our woods are dangerous now."

"I am here, safe. The amount of sickness alarmed me. Deep winter hasn't arrived, yet already so many had wet lung. I hope I've harvested enough for this wet-cold season. The villagers gave me gifts, dried foods, herbs, and so many things. I couldn't carry them all. We must send braves to collect them."

"I will see to that. You look healthy and strong…but tired," Running Bear said looking into his mate's eyes. "Where did you sleep last night?"

"In the cave of my childhood, a special place. I'll show it

to you someday." WolfShe felt searing heat rise in her face when Running Bear kissed her cheek, his longing obvious. "Yes, I am well and strong. How are our elders?"

"Healthy…because you ordered us to eat salal berry cakes."

"Good. I will prepare more. I dried many berries. Do you have more *oolichan* oil for me?"

"Bladders full. Mother will help. Give me the baskets," he said, lifting the first one. Running Bear leaned over to grab the other but stopped midway to nuzzle WolfShe's neck, rubbing up and down the warmth under her loose hair. He smiled. "Let's go home."

They walked, catching up on village news, but WolfShe said nothing to Running Bear about oozing sore illness… or her wolf.

"How was their summer catch?" Running Bear asked, positioning the baskets on his shoulders.

"Good, they said. Late summer they smoked salmon day and night. So many Bear People wandered into the village to feast on salmon bits that they moved the fires to another area. The bears left fat and shiny. They gave me baskets of dried salmon, enough to see us through the winter, but I left them at the healing house."

"WolfShe, don't do this again—never travel alone. I'm your mate. I will escort you."

WolfShe disliked Running Bear commanding her as if he could make her obey by reminding her of mate duties. "You can collect my gifts whenever you like. Everything is stored in the longhouse—dried bulbs, berries, smoked salmon, a cedar box for storing medicines, dried medicine plants, cedar-cloth, and even a fine coat for me. Things I share with you, my mate, and with my village, gifts given to honor my work. Medicine woman work is not like other work, Running Bear. You know that. You know me…a little. You accepted me. Do not tell me what to do."

"WolfShe, everyone shows their appreciation for your healing work with gifts. I show you by protecting you, giving you a family. I think of your safety. I do not order you like other braves order their women. You cannot say that."

WolfShe smiled and looked away. "A man called me *witchdoctor.* I told him I use no spells, only herbs. He didn't believe me. He had heard healing spirits work with me and have since the Great Flood."

"Do they?"

The look on Running Bear's face made WolfShe laugh. "You know Ama taught me. I have no spirit helpers, not even ancestors I can call on."

"What about wolf? Our people say Wolf Totem spirits help and guard you. Now since Three-Legged has disappeared, they say he resides in the Land of Mists…and always has."

"Three-Legged runs free with his pack. He's my brother, not a spirit guardian."

"Your wolf has become a legend, campfire story."

WolfShe felt uncomfortable. She shifted his attention. "I heard something that scared me. News of a terrible illness, one I have never seen. The man who told me called it *oozing sore disease.* Have you heard of it?"

"No."

"It starts with a fever, body pains, and swelling throat. The skin turns red and erupts with raised bumps, first on the face and hands, then on the chest and back. Fever and horrible chills come and go. Sores spread sap and more sores come. The person dies in three or four sunrises. Running Bear, no one lives through this, even the strongest whaler dies."

"Every time?"

"Yes…everyone who comes near the sick person. All die. Evil flows into them from the sores that boil, ooze, and spread. Some die very fast. Others die more slowly…and in great pain. Men, women, children."

"Where is this disease?"

"The traveler told me it started on the mainland, with traders and trappers and spread to the north coast. He said he hasn't seen it for himself. Otherwise he would be dead."

"Sounds like a firepit story, a horrible one. Some must live."

"Running Bear, the fear in his words felt true. I don't know how to prepare for such an illness. I haven't the skill. He said many have died from it, whole villages in the Far North islands."

Running Bear took her by the hand. She felt his warmth travel through her cold trembling hands to steady and warm her heart. Running Bear said calmly, "We will find out more and prepare. No one has spoken of this. Could there be poison in the water? A rotten catch?"

"I don't know."

"Forget illness for now. I have a surprise. Mother made you a gift: boots, elk hide lined with rabbit fur. Soft and warm. You can walk through water in them, she oiled them so well."

"Why did she do that for me?"

"So cold ground won't enter your feet and chill our baby."

"Baby?"

"The baby she expects us to make soon, when buds form and sun touches the ground."

"Great Spirit decides what and when…not your mother."

"She put fertility charms in our section of the longhouse. She said they will work by blossom time."

"She's been busy. Maybe she should have another baby. Your little brother is five now. She needs a baby to care for."

"Don't you?"

"No, I have you."

⁂

WolfShe settled back into longhouse life. She continued to use Ama's cabin to prepare and store medicines, but she also used the cabin near their longhouse for food and other potions that required daily attention. She took her dried herbs and berries out into the early spring sun to inspect them for mold, fungus, and rot, pleased they looked healthy. Careful drying ensured they would. She hung baskets of medicine plants in the healing house, and when Running Bear's men returned with her gifts from Wolf Fang, she added those to her stores.

She walked from longhouse to longhouse to inspect what the women had put aside, on her recommendation, in their home medicine baskets, and felt better about preparations for early spring illnesses, except for oozing sore disease. She agreed with Running Bear, no one they knew and could trust had seen the disease, oozing sore. How could they when no one lived to tell? WolfShe began to think the description a mistake. Poison hemlock had been bartered, at times, as wild carrot. Families, not recognizing it, ate it. The terrible rash, vomiting, and seizing of limbs would scare anyone into thinking it was the disease the traveler described.

WolfShe trained a young girl, Sitka, she had known from River Bend Village to assist her with gathering herbs and preparing tonics, salves, medicine teas, ailing-stomach chewing gum, pleasure gum, and sarsaparilla water. Eventually her apprentice would work with poison plants, if and when WolfShe approved. Ama had waited eight years before she taught WolfShe to harvest and use poisonous plants—especially hemlock, death-cap mushroom, and death lily. WolfShe planned to wait even longer with Sitka.

WolfShe called out, "Sitka, reline the baskets with dried willow leaves and layer the medicines between cedar towels. Set aside two large baskets for wound dressing—poultice strips, and bandages. Take one to the medicine longhouse. Tomorrow we'll make more salal cakes. The sun shines for our work, but clouds build over the mountain and a chill wind blows. We must work fast."

She watched Sitka work, thinking her quick and careful. She has the kind of skill I had when I was young, she thought. "Continue, Sitka, and you'll make a good medicine woman, but it will take many summers. Let's see if your interest blossoms, or wilts. You may think more about braves, and less about medicines. Dedication and skill, every medicine woman must have both."

Her own words rang in her head, making WolfShe question if she had the stamina and skill to face oozing sore disease. The fear in the traveler's voice haunted her. What demon could cause everyone to die? If it's true no one survives, then no healer survives either. Then how to stop such illness? She thought about the story of Star Child, the ancient one sent by Great Spirit to teach the first people which plants to eat, which were poisonous, and which were medicine. Medicine knowledge had started with Star Child. She wondered if the ancient one had known of oozing sore disease remedies.

Possibly when the world was young and Great Spirit commanded the first people to make large canoes because

rains would come to destroy much of the earth, Great Spirit
had sent the rain to test the people, as the elders taught.
Or was it to wash away oozing sore disease since demons
can't swim?

Great Spirit instructed the first people to go up the
mountain and build huge rafts of cedar logs and lash them
together with cedar ropes. Great Spirit ordered them to tie
the boats to large boulders, and when the rains came with
no break and the land began to sink, to load up and cut free.
Great Spirit wanted to find out who was clever and strong
enough to survive. When they showed their abilities, Great
Spirit chose those people to create the tribes of men and
women to live on the cleansed earth, to start anew.

The story vibrated in WolfShe's vision like a fragile
branch buffeted by strong current. She thought she heard
her mother's voice conclude the story with a whisper and a
prayer: *Be strong, be brave, work hard to please Great Spirit.*
WolfShe saw her child-self slumped on the ground—sad,
bewildered, and angry—asking, Maaha, why would Great
Spirit test his children with a flood?

WolfShe shook and glanced over at Sitka to see a dark
snake slither near her feet. She shouted, "Jump!" Sitka
looked down at the dirt floor and stared at WolfShe. "Continue your work, Sitka," WolfShe said, seeing the confusion
in the girl's eyes. "I'm going for a walk."

WolfShe knew the sighting meant something, but what?
She wanted to hike alone to high meadow to look for a special herb, one only medicine women use, a vision-clearing
herb. She crossed the river on the rope bridge, bouncing on
steady feet, and hiked uphill, hoping to find salal berries in
the sheltered area where the boulders enclosed hot spring
water bubbling up from the earth. Steam from the rocks

encouraged plants to produce early. Their tender leaves, worth collecting, enhanced broth flavor.

Above Ama's cabin, she entered Dead Warrior Forest, where spirits of dead warriors dwelled, angry from their last battle, waiting to fight with anyone who tread their land. WolfShe said blessings on ceremony days for them. She knew they would let her pass, as they always had. Warring spirits only disturb those who carry anger and hatred in their heart. She carried neither, although even the slightest amount attracts them.

She found a sheltered bush full of slightly shriveled blue salal berries. She hadn't expected to find so many, but wedged between hot rocks, hard for animals to reach, and protected from cold weather, the bush thrived. Some of the leaves, tender enough for medicine tea for stomach and throat fire, she picked and threw into her medicine basket; larger ones she gathered for flavoring fish broth. Among the berry bushes she spotted the tiny white flower she sought for vision-clearing, withered but potent. She knew Black Snake could not haunt her after she drank tea made from the seeds.

The chill morning air warmed. WolfShe rested next to the bubbling spring, despite its bitter smell that made her nose twitch. She leaned back against the warm rocks, nibbled some berries, and dozed to the gentle sound of dancing water. When she woke, the sun had lowered. She jumped up to cut limbs for a dragging frame to carry cedar boughs home for ceremonies. Her knife skipped and stumbled across the bark, but she made a frame of two long branches with shorter pieces for cross supports. She notched the poles and tied the frame, leaving enough cedar braid for a handle, tied her gathering baskets to the dragging frame, and wiped her purple-stained hands. The effort had taken more time than she thought. If she hurried, she figured she could cross the forest in daylight, avoiding the area where rotting logs littered the way and angry braves grumbled. She could reach home before sunset.

A slight breeze tickled the forest. Shadows danced. The air, filled with pine, spruce, and cedar scents, cleared WolfShe's fatigue. The frame caught on a moss-covered branch, throwing her off balance. She stopped to right it. In the damp ground, she saw uneven scars on the forest floor. She stepped closer to study the impressions: deep Two-Legged ones made from hard-edge moccasins. *Not my people.* She scanned the forest. She abandoned her load to follow the uneven tracks. In a muddy spot, she dropped to her knees and sniffed. She jumped. She withdrew her knife, her heart thundering in her ears.

She continued following the trail, stopping to listen, sniff, and touch the earth. *Fresh, less than a half-day,* she realized. *Where does he go?* Her stomach knotted. She couldn't speak his name for fear of drawing him to her. Dead warrior spirits overhead grew angry; they rattled their bows. Wind came up, branches scraped, night owls hooted and flew away. WolfShe sang a protection song Ama had taught her when she was very young, a song about girls that looked like birds and could fly away from danger. The song and the thought of Ama soothed her. The warriors settled.

She noticed a shallow mound sticking up from disturbed pine needles. WolfShe grabbed a stick. She brushed away the matted debris. A *metul* trap, teeth ready to bite, stared at her. She stepped back. Warrior spirits rushed at her. They pricked her skin with sharp arrow points that stung like bees. Black forms swirled in the boughs, shaking

     D Y A N   D U B O I S

the trees, and screeching. She sang Ama's song aloud. The wind died. Branches stilled.

WolfShe jammed a thick branch into the trap, hitting the whalebone support. The jaws bit through the wood, sending bark shards flying. She didn't stay to bury this one. She followed the trail deeper into the forest. In the distance, she heard a wolf. She recognized the howl: Three-Legged.

She couldn't leave the forest in dim light. Pale Face never set only one trap, she knew. She must find them, for her sake and for wolf's. He had a pattern, large sweeps in a circle with several set along the arc. She retraced her steps to the trap. She picked up the snapped whalebone support, sharp enough for a weapon at close range, and stuck it into her waist tie. She covered the closed trap with dirt and covered it with needles, leaving a large, visible mound. She swung wide in an arc. She couldn't smell the trapper's foul odor, rotting flesh and skunk spray, so she assumed he couldn't be close. The thought boosted her courage and calmed the angry warriors.

From the corner of her eye, she saw shadowy forms dart tree to tree. I track him, warriors track me, she thought. I hope they fight on my side. She came to dense trees carpeted by ferns, terrain she knew Pale Face liked for traps. Wolves walk without seeing beneath the fronds. She picked her steps carefully, surveying every bend in the bracken before she moved, poking with a stick. Dim light flattened the impressions in the ground. She crouched, waving the stick in front of her to separate the ferns before she stepped.

WolfShe struck something hard. She shoved back the ferns. Another open jaw *metul*. She tapped it, heard the ping. She bent the bracken to mark the place and backtracked to find a heavy branch. She dragged it back, walked it upright near the trap, and positioning herself to the side, spread her feet, braced, and pushed. The huge branch crashed forward onto the trap, the whalebone support cracked, and the forest rang with *metul* biting *metul*.

WolfShe staggered backward with fear, disgust, and fatigue. Her stomach rolled. Death does not come fast. "Suffering lasts long," she whispered. Hatred rose in her like a burning fire. Her thoughts hissed like broth hitting firepit rocks. Sweat poured from her forehead.

CHAPTER THIRTEEN

Final Contact

WolfShe realized she shouldn't continue in the dark. Fading light has a way of distorting things; shadows emphasize and conceal. She could be the animal Pale Face watches die. WolfShe had no idea how many traps he had set, but even one could end her. She must hurry. She worried for Wolf People since they travel at night. Their eyes detect the slightest motion, a help for hunting but not for detecting a stationary trap masked by forest duff. She prayed for the wolves to go higher up-mountain and for her to walk safe steps.

Swinging wide to leave the woods, she intended to follow the stream—not her usual way home—but her safest. Pale Face set traps in the forest, not the meadow. She heard a wolf howl. The cry constricted her heart and made her arm hairs stand: a howl of warning, she sighed, a cry of malice, the death-battle sound. She heard a responding howl farther away. She understood: Three-Legged's in danger.

WolfShe increased her pace in the distorted play of light and shadow. She ran toward the sound. Jumping a log, sprinting to open ground, she froze when she spotted a small rise in the earth. She leapt sideways, her foot grazing a hard edge, and landed beyond the mound with a thud. She jumped up and grabbed a broken branch to smash the forest duff. Bark and splinters flew when the *metul* jaw bit.

Another howl shattered the deepening gray and ripped through the air like lightning, searing her confidence. WolfShe felt her world slow to spring sap. She couldn't move. A low, guttural growl raced along the ground toward her. The predator's smell stunned her. She tried to *think-speak* with Three-Legged. She collapsed on her haunches, flattened, and lay hidden in the bracken. The evening breeze shifted.

He must see me, she thought. She held her breath and studied the shadow forest. She heard a slight grunt from behind. Pale Face charged, swinging a rope that landed on WolfShe's head. She jumped; the rope slipped. She circled him, knife drawn. She moved like a badger—aggressive spurts, halts, turns—and drew closer and then jumped away, luring him, tiring him, confusing him. He could not keep up. She intended to run just ahead, barely out of reach, to distract him from her wolf. She looked at him. She gasped.

Three-Legged, a racing black shadow against twilight gray, fangs exposed, lips curled, crouched behind Pale Face, ready to spring, growling like a demon. The trapper half-turned to look. WolfShe rushed him. He knocked her sideways. She fell. Pale Face charged the wolf with a long-blade knife. WolfShe screamed, "Run!" Wolf leapt into shadow. Pale Face rushed the darkness, his gutting knife held in front of his chest. They disappeared.

A screech ripped the forest. She bolted toward the sound. A horrifying scream followed. WolfShe couldn't see Three-Legged, but she heard his panting, moaning, snarling. She ran his direction. A deep growl reverberated in her chest. Then a chilling shriek.

WolfShe found wolf crouched over the trapper's writhing body, fangs bared, ears flattened. She stepped closer. She squinted to focus. *Metul* teeth pierced Pale Face's shoulder near the neck. Black blood gushed from the wound. She yelled at the trapper. He didn't answer...or move. She grabbed his head and tried to pull his neck from the trap. She used his gutting knife to pry open the *metul* teeth. She couldn't. Pale Face whimpered like a pup, opened his eyes, and looked into hers. He twitched violently and fell slack. WolfShe backed away from his body.

Three-Legged stood over the trapper, growling. He sniffed the warm blood. WolfShe's stomach rolled. She turned and vomited on the bracken. She let out a terrifying scream that caused elk to bugle alarm, cougars to screech, and wolves to howl in fear. Three-Legged hopped to her and rubbed his muzzle along her arm and cheek. He raised his muzzle to the night sky, let out a low, solitary wail...and disappeared.

※ ※ ※

WolfShe didn't know how long she had remained, stunned and motionless, collapsed next to the body. Through eyes distorted by tears, she saw torch lights. She stood on wobbly legs and limped over to rest her back against a tree.

WolfShe heard Running Bear yelling, "WolfShe, where are you? Shout."

"Here. Over here," WolfShe called out in a thready, inaudible voice. When their footfalls drew close, she cleared her throat and screamed, "*Metul* traps. Don't run!"

WolfShe   171

The braves drew closer, sweeping torches low in front of them, scanning the ground, picking their steps. Running Bear rushed to her, grabbing WolfShe with such force they fell into the tree. They swayed in each other's arms.

"You killed Pale Face with his own trap?" Running Bear asked, his voice wavering.

"No. He did."

"Is he alone? Are there others?"

"I don't know. I saw no one else. *Metul* traps could be anywhere. We must leave this place."

"Did he hurt you? Blood's on you."

"His blood. I tried to free him, Running Bear. I couldn't. *Metul* teeth bit his neck."

"Stay here," he said bracing her against the trunk. Running Bear rushed over to inspect the trapper's body. He shouted to a brave, "Hold a torch overhead. What happened to his face?"

WolfShe forced herself to go nearer and look at the death grimace. She studied his face, pitted with ridges of scarred flesh circling sunken wells of shadow. "Hold the torch closer," she commanded the brave. "His face looks…" A sickening feeling overcame WolfShe. "She screamed, "Step away!"

Running Bear stepped back and spat like he had tasted something foul. "He looks like he's been burned."

"He wasn't burned by flame. He survived a terrible illness that destroyed his face, ate his skin."

"What illness, WolfShe?"

"One I've heard of. Poison demons erupt from the skin in oozing sores. A traveler called it *oozing sore disease.*"

"You told me of oozing sore disease, WolfShe, but you said no one lived."

WolfShe's voice trembled. "I was told the body…cannot survive. Disease demons eat until the body dies and then they move to the next, to whoever has touched the person. No one survives."

She looked at her hands and felt the north wind blow freezing rain through her. Her fingers turned to ice. Running Bear reached out to hold her. She jumped back.

"Do not touch me. All of you, stay away…from me and from his body."

"I must wash him off you. He's poison. Braves, back away. Do not go near that body," Running Bear shouted and removed his tunic to throw on top of the body.

"We can't leave him, Running Bear. The skin demons will kill the forest animals."

"You two, stay here for the night, guard the body but don't go near," Running Bear said, motioning to the braves. "Make a large fire. Keep animals away. Stand guard. Other Pale Faces may come. Be ready to kill on sight. You walk with us," he said to the youngest brave. "I will return at dawn to burn the body."

Running Bear, the brave, and WolfShe walked to the hot spring creek. The brave positioned further away from them, scanned the terrain. WolfShe stripped down and washed while Running Bear chanted prayers in the four directions. WolfShe said nothing. She acted like a fish tangled in a net. She thrashed; she quaked in the warm water. Her body rose in violent waves of revulsion, churned, tossed, and righted before the next wave began. She couldn't control her shaking. She moved away from Running Bear's waiting arms when she stepped out of the creek to dry off. Running Bear threw her the young brave's tunic to wrap herself in.

She spoke in a raspy whisper. "Oozing sore disease. Do not touch me. You wash now."

Running Bear flared. "Why did you try to free him? He meant to kill you and Wolf People, especially your Three-Legged. I thought Pale Face had died. I was sure of it."

"He returned from over the sea, I was told. I didn't believe it. I thought him dead. He came from a land of no sun. That's what I was told. His kind are pale like fish belly with no color in their eyes."

Running Bear stepped into the hot stream to wash off. "My grandfather said something to me about that shipwreck when he first saw *metul* as a very young man. He said some called it Great Spirit's gift, but he warned them to stay away from those pale people and their *metul*. He said no good would come from them. Grandfather believed that *metul* ring had slipped into our world through a demon gate from Shadow Land. It was some sort of curse they brought. He warned something worse might slip through."

"Running Bear, I will stay alone at Ama's cabin until the full moon withers. I will follow sacred ceremony, do cleansing sweats. Oozing sore demons must not invade our land. Care for yourself and our family. Before we part, hold your hands in flame. Do it now." She told the brave to approach and hold the torch. "Run your hands through the flame. The hairs will burn before the skin. Do it as long as you can, then remove them, let them cool, and do it again. The demons will die. Fire purifies."

Running Bear moved his hands back and forth through the flames, slowly, five times before he jerked them out. "I can't do more."

"When you get home, rub bear grease on your hands, hold them in flame for as long as you can, but don't burn

     D Y A N   D U B O I S

them. The skin will redden. Then wash with wormwood water, dry, and spread a thin layer of spruce gum on your hands. Wrap them in cedar-cloth. Put spruce gum wraps on for two sunrises. I will do the same at Ama's. On the third, you will be clean, and with Great Spirit's blessing, I will cleanse also."

"Let me stay with you at Ama's. We can help each other."

"No. I must be alone. I have sacred methods Ama taught me that only I can witness. Send no one to me. Drop off food and firewood in the cedar grove by the cabin. I will come to you when I am clean, not before."

The three walked to Ama's cabin, in a single line, silence separating their worlds. When WolfShe turned to say goodbye, Running Bear pleaded to stay with her, but she ordered him away saying, "Medicine Woman of Wolf Totem commands you to leave me for the good of the village. You must obey. I will come to you if I can. Burn the body at dawn and scorch the surrounding earth."

⁕

WolfShe made a large fire in the ceremonial firepit outside Ama's cabin. She raked burning cedar over her skin. She washed with boiling water and scrubbed her skin with lichen dipped in salmonberry bark tea. She slathered her body with charcoal powder and deer fat salve. Although the night was cold, she wore no clothes. She kept fires roaring in the cabin and outside where she walked around the circle of stones in prayer until stars slipped from the milky sky. Retreating inside, she burned cedar logs and boughs to cleanse the air. Ama's cabin became her sweat lodge. She poured sacred herbs into water and splashed them onto hot rocks. She fell asleep, naked, by the firepit, the air heavy with incense smoke and steam. When she woke, she began again.

She listened when she heard men's voices beyond the cabin on their way to dispose of the body. "Good," she said. No one approached her door, as ordered. She knew Running Bear would lead the braves in sweat lodge cleanses. The women would hold their own sacred ceremonies. She felt the tribe's prayers swirl around her. WolfShe passed the day in prayer, fasting on salmonberry bark tea. She didn't hear the men return, but when she looked out after sunset, wood and a food basket waited for her. She broke her fast at night to begin it again the next sunrise.

WolfShe prayed, sweated, and fasted. On the third night, a large honey-ochre moon rose through the tangled tree branches, casting long shadows on the ground. She remembered, as a child, how she had jumped from one shadow to another, so the moon couldn't catch her. She believed if it did, the Great Flood would come again. Ama had made her stop when WolfShe explained why she jumped shadows. But WolfShe continued the practice—out of Ama's sight—long after she promised not to. And tonight, she would observe her ritual again.

She walked in full-moon glow to look at the dried meadow grass stalks that stood up from the earth like golden arrows. On the forest border of Ama's small meadow, tree fingers reached out to grab the arrows. She avoided their shadows. WolfShe breathed in the fresh, cold air. She laughed. She felt strong. She had defeated the demons. Her skin was clear. Her thoughts were calm. Soon, she could return to Running Bear.

She shouted to the trees, "Pale Face trapper will never hurt Wolf People again. Great Spirit blessed us and took the

     Dyan Dubois

diseased Pale Face away." She danced in the chilly moonlight. A familiar howl stopped her; she jerked to a stop. The howl turned to a whimper and grew closer. "Wolf?" she called to the night.

Three-Legged loped from the shadows into the moonlit meadow. She grew afraid. The wolf was too large to be *her* wolf. She stumbled backward and started to run for the cabin. She turned, blinked, and looked again. Three-Legged walked toward her, upright on hind legs.

WolfShe shouted, "What demon comes? This is sacred ground." The wolf lowered to all fours and trotted toward her in his uneven gate. He halted in front of her. WolfShe held her breath. Too much fasting? My mind plays tricks. "Friend? I see you now as you were. You've come back to me. The demon Pale Face is gone…forever."

WolfShe danced with her hands lifted to the sky, gathering stars with her outstretched fingers. She danced on the golden arrows, bending them to the ground, and laughed. Three-Legged pranced beside her, as steady as any four-legged animal. When he rose up on his hinds, she laughed. "So now you dance like a Two-Legged?" She ran her hand down his back, feeling the crisp cool air in his fur.

Owls hooted from the trees. A halo of mist rose from the golden arrows and swirled around WolfShe and Three-Legged. The two of them raced like children across the hard ground, faster than the wind, brighter than the sun…until a familiar voice called.

WolfShe stopped abruptly, digging in with her toes to keep from toppling over. Her body rocked back and forth. She settled to a full stop. From the mist, she saw a figure approach.

"Ama!"

"Yes, WolfShe. I have come with a gift," she said and pointed to three swirling vapor figures, the smallest jumping up and down, waving her hands in excitement. "You may speak, but do not touch."

WolfShe choked seeing the forms develop into Maaha's face, her father with his broad smile, and baby sister with wide eyes, smiling.

Her father's deep voice sounded like a flute on the night air. "Daughter, you have done well. Great Spirit blessed you; and you, us. Your healing work helped our tribe unite again in the Land of Mists. We stand as your ancestors, ready to assist you in the work Great Spirit has assigned you. Long have we heard your laments. Let your heart grow light. We are never far from you. We are People of the Wolf. Wolf is your totem, our family ancestral totem. We had told you when you were our child, but like wind that blows quietly and disappears, the memory faded. Your Ama guessed correctly. Wolves in the forest guarded and nurtured you until she found you. The wolf beside you has traveled many lands, many ages, with our totem. He and his league, called Justice Wolves, come from long-ago creation. Wolf, stand now, repeat your pledge."

WolfShe watched Three-Legged rise on his hinds and walk toward her. She looked up at his towering height.

"In every age of human life, a woman child will be born with healing knowledge, and in every age a wolf of my kind shall guard her. So Great Spirit promised. Spat out from the original Great Flood as whale, our kind became wolf on land to create a new understanding between human and animal. We live in harmony of purpose. I come from a long line of Justice Wolves devoted to service, companionship, and protection of healers."

   DYAN DUBOIS

The mist began to thin. WolfShe called out, "I have many questions, please stay."

Ama spoke. "Continue your work, child. We will greet you at your appointed time, in the Land of Mists. WolfShe of Wolf Totem, be well and listen to the wind. We are with you."

WolfShe glowed like a million stars filled her belly. She felt her mother's kiss fall lightly on her face, her sister's little hand squeeze her own, and her father's kind touch on her cheek.

The mist lifted. The meadow flooded with the amber light of the full, setting moon. Beside her, Three-Legged balanced on his good legs, leaning against WolfShe. His soft fur warmed her.

THE END

www.ingramcontent.com/pod-product-compliance
Lightning Source LLC
Chambersburg PA
CBHW022208050726
47590CB00002B/702